THE PLAYER

MEN OF WARHAWKS- BOOK 2

JACQUIE BIGGAR

WAVEFRONT PUBLISHING

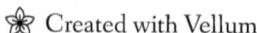

My Girl

My Girl has everything to love in a novel: hunky and handsome cowboys with soft hearts, second chance romances, cute kids and some secrets and suspense thrown in.

— COLORADO COWGIRL

Skating on Thin Ice

Jacquie Biggar has done it again. I have yet another new book boyfriend—Mac Wanowski, captain of the Victoria WarHawks hockey team.

— WRITESTER

The Lady Said No

"The Lady Said No is an **addictive mystery** filled with **cagy characters** with the backdrop of the greatest horse race known to man."

— AMAZON REVIEWER

*As a proud Canadian, I would like to dedicate this book
to our hockey heroes- past and present.*

Hockey is not a one-man show; it's a team effort. If you don't work as a team - even if one or two guys aren't working - you're not going to win. That's the way it is.

— GUY LAFLEUR

INTRODUCTION

Sometimes, love happens when we least expect it...

NHL defenseman Roy Donaldson lives for the game. When an ex-girlfriend/stalker causes trouble for the team, Roy gets benched.

And the only way he can return to the rotation...? Accept help from sassy, sexy PA Patience Kennedy.

Patience is one step away from a junior partnership-- all she needs to do is restore a sullen, annoying, attractive hockey player's image.

Shouldn't be too hard, right?

PREFACE

"A couple of days ago, just after we arrived, your girl-friend made an announcement—ex," she hurried to correct, flicking him a glance beneath her lashes. Yep, definitely, not a happy camper.

His teeth ground together audibly. "What kind of *announcement*, Kennedy?"

He used her last name like a curse. Was it wrong she found it kind of hot? "Umm, well, Olivia did an interview with the *Times Colonist* and declared she's pregnant—with your child. She says that's the real reason you dumped her and that when she told you about it you threatened her if she didn't get an abortion."

It wasn't true, of course it wasn't. Still... Patience slid her glasses back on and his grim face came into sharp focus. "Did you know she was pregnant, Roy?"

His fists slammed down on the table, upsetting the water bottle. "Seriously? Is that what you think? That I would turn away a woman in need? One carrying my child—which is bullshit, by the way. I use protection. Every. Time." He rose and clenched his hands on the back of his chair. "She's going to ruin me, isn't she? How am I supposed to beat this?"

The bleakness in his eyes cut her heart to ribbons. He'd just taken a body slam and it was her fault. She could have, should have, prepared him for this setback. What kind of personal assistant left their client to wander around in the dark? It was her duty to ferret out anything detrimental to his image and counter it before it could gain traction. She'd failed.

And that pissed her off.

"Okay—" she said, righting his water bottle and rising to meet him eye to chest, "new plan. We're going to change tactics. Instead of ignoring the problem, you're going to face it head on. What do you call it? A face-off. Yeah," she lifted a finger and shook it, "a face-off. She's the opposing team and you're going to do what you do best—beat her at her own game."

His brows had slowly risen at her outburst and now those firm lips quirked. "Whoa, remind me not to get on your bad side—you're a tiger in disguise, Patience Kennedy."

Heat suffused her cheeks. "I'm sorry, Roy. I let you

down. If you want to fire me, I totally understand." She refused to lower her chin, though it was the hardest thing she'd ever done.

Roy shook his head and moved around the table to grasp said chin. The pad of his thumb feathered her lower lip before coming to rest along her jawline. Her silly heart performed cartwheels at the intimacy. She froze, everything within her leaning into the touch, and waited. Wanted. Anticipated.

"I'm not letting you go just yet," he murmured. "We have a contract."

His words had the undesired effect of cooling her ardor. He was right, they had a contract. And if she wanted to keep her career, she'd better remember that.

Just then, her cell phone buzzed from its spot on the table, saving her an awkward retreat. She took a step back, figuratively and literally, and turned the screen so she could read the text: *thirty seconds to airtime.*

"It's the station, they're ready for you." She kept her gaze down, opening the computer and dragging it out of sleep-mode. Sadly enough, she could see similarities between herself and the machine. Time for both of them to wake up.

"Patience..." Roy looked at her with something like regret. "I didn't mean to suggest anything."

Could her face get any hotter? "I know. Could we

get down to business, please? My advice is to shoot straight from the hip. If someone asks you about... you know, Olivia, tell them the truth. Diplomatically, of course," she hastened to add.

He hesitated, then nodded and resumed his seat. "Sure, if that's what you really want." He looked at her meaningfully before turning to the computer. "Let's get this over with."

Feeling like she'd lost something precious, Patience keyed in a response to the waiting announcer: *We're ready*.

"And we're back with WarHawks defenseman Roy Donaldson. Roy, are you ready for your next caller?"

Roy locked eyes with Patience. "Bring it on, Sam."

"Great. Caller number two, you're live on KPLY Sportsdesk. What would you like to ask our hockey hero today?"

There was a brief spurt of static, then a woman's voice came through, sharp as cut glass. "I want to ask my fiancé when he plans to quit running like scared chickenshit and step up to the blueline—the one on my pregnancy test, that is."

Patience's eyes widened even as Roy's expression turned arctic cold.

Olivia.

Men of Warhawks Book 2

The
Player

USA Today Bestselling Author
JACQUIE BIGGAR

Roy Donaldson tightened his gloves and adjusted his helmet before giving the WarHawks' goalie a nod. Time to get down to business. He dropped into defensive position, ignoring the catcalls coming from the Edmonton fans. It was always like this when they played away from home; he'd gotten used to it and actually even kind of liked the anonymous insults and whistles. It only spurred him to try harder. Beat the odds.

The puck dropped, signaling the beginning of the third period. Their team captain, Mac Wanowski, stole it away from the Oilers and passed it off to their right wingman, Cooper. Coop headed down the ice like his skates were on rails, the puck nestled like a baby in the pocket of his stick. Wanowski stayed off his flank, keeping the Oilers' center busy dodging his moves.

Meanwhile, Lazlo protected his left to chants from the crowd.

Roy moved up, prepared for a lightning-fast backward pass, Coop's trademark move. They were close to the attack zone now, the tension thicker than the ice beneath his feet. The sharp slap of his stick sending the puck shooting across to Lazlo and then Lazlo's back to Coop combined with the announcer's excited dialogue, the flash from the jumbotron's big screen, the scents of ammonia and popcorn and the musty eau de cologne all hockey players wore with their sweaty gear. He lived for this; the all-encompassing thrill of the game. Win or lose—Winning preferably—it didn't matter, as long as he had the WarHawks.

A roar from the crowd shifted his attention from Lazlo and Coop to Mac and the captain from the other team. Gloves had come off and they were shoving each other hard against the boards, the thick plexiglass rattling with the force of their blows. If Mac messed up that bad leg of his again, the new coach would have his head. Where the hell were the refs?

The thought no sooner crossed his mind than whistles screamed. He was too far down ice to be much help, so he skidded to a halt and glanced up at the clock to see how much time was left in the period; fifteen minutes, plenty of time to teach these guys a lesson—even with the penalty. They were one goal down at the moment, just the way he liked it. They played better from behind; more incentive to kick some Oiler asses. They'd barely made the playoffs last season after Wanowski blew out his knee. And then, when all that crap with Coach Harris and Doc Edwards went down, he'd half expected the team to get kicked out of the league, but here they were, new-found notoriety and all.

Lazlo had gotten into the thick of it and it was taking three referees to pull him and Mac away from the Oiler player. It would take time to run the replays to determine who was at fault.

He glanced up at the jumbotron, expecting to see the fight in slo-mo. Instead, the screen was filled with a shot of a woman holding a giant sign in the stands. Hearts and kisses framed the words, *Be Mine, Roy Donaldson.* He shook his head. Exhibitionists abounded at these events, but he'd never understood the draw. If he wanted to court a lover, it wasn't going to be in the midst of a crowd of strangers. He preferred a king-sized bed and silk sheets when wooing his woman.

The camera focused on the crazy-eyed gaze of a dark-haired woman and Roy swore.

Olivia.

His gut clenched. Shit, what was *she* doing here? The woman was a menace. She'd stalked him until he'd been forced to take out a restraining order against her. Yet, there she was, smiling into the camera as though she had every right.

Son-of-a-...

"Samson, you playing, or what?" Cole yelled from the goalie's net.

Roy's gaze remained fixed on the screen, willing his eyes to be deceiving him. But he was right, it was the woman he'd stupidly thought himself in love with. Olivia had hid her face now, as though realizing she'd screwed up. Welcome to his world. The repercussions would be all over the news broadcasts by morning. He'd have to find someone to handle the fallout. And why was he thinking about the aftermath when his life had just exploded in his face? Save the anger for later, when he was alone. It wasn't like it was the first time he'd been betrayed, after all.

He turned his back on the jumbotron. "Ya, man, let's play."

*O*ne *month later*

Patience Kennedy sat next to her boss and watched the fuming man below them swish swishing from one end of the ice to the other, lap after lap. Even though tension rolled off him in waves, he was mesmerizing to watch. Powerful. Graceful. Potent.

She'd seen enough pictures of him to know he had an intensity that probably stood him in good stead on the rink. It didn't translate well for publicity, however, which is why she was currently freezing her caboodle off on this bench. She'd warned Linda she had no experience with sports—her thighs quivered at the mere thought—but it didn't seem to matter. Linda wanted what Linda wanted and she'd decided Patience was perfect for this client.

Roy Donaldson.

The Victoria WarHawks' golden boy. Winner of the James Norris Memorial Trophy for best defense. An all-star athlete who'd just been propositioned on national television by a kooky ex-girlfriend, creating a media storm.

Donaldson wasn't playing his 'A' game right now and it was costing the team. They'd lost the last four games and had dropped in the rankings. Any more losses and the playoffs were over for them. Sayonara to their juicy bonuses.

"Did you hear a word I just said?" Linda asked, tapping her pen against her notepad. She didn't trust the internet; everything was done old school. Funny, considering she owned one of the premiere PR firms in the country.

"The guy driving the Zamboni could hear you." Patience smiled to soften the words. "Yes, I know the GM is an old friend and there's more than meets the eye to the story. I'll do my best, but this is out of my comfort zone." So far out it could be in another stratosphere.

"That's all I'm asking." Linda turned a shrewd gaze her way. "Besides, a little bird told me you think it's time I gave you a promotion, maybe even junior partnership?"

Patience cringed. She was going to kill Tammy.

Her best friend (and Linda's sister) meant well, but what they chatted about during a Friday night wine-and-a-movie binge was sacred. "To be fair, it's been five years and I feel I've brought something to your business. My clients—except the Mastersons, who hate everyone—all left glowing reviews on the website, which I helped update, by the way."

"And I appreciate, thank you." Linda's eyes sparked with suppressed amusement. "No wonder I hired you. You could sell coffee in a teahouse. That's why I need you to handle Mr. Donaldson's publicity. The WarHawks are in a vulnerable position. Negative exposure reflects badly on the league and they can't have that. It all comes down to finances. The NHL works hard to portray a positive experience for their fans—and penalize the players who jeopardize that image."

She held up a bejeweled hand before Patience could jump to her new client's defense. "Before you say it, I know. It's not fair. Mr. Donaldson is the fall-guy for a situation not of his own making, but that's the nature of the beast. He's not as important as the team—which makes our boy down there," she nodded to the skater shooting slapshots into a net at the far end of the ice, "expendable."

Patience frowned. She didn't even know the guy and already felt sorry for him. The tabloids had been merciless, running the story of the dropped girlfriend as though he'd committed a major betrayal. Personally, she was surprised it hadn't turned into old news already, but it seemed as though a smear campaign had been launched against Mr. Donaldson. Paparazzi followed him everywhere, snapping photos of a grim, forbidding face—not exactly family-friendly viewing. Trouble was, he preferred his privacy, but he wasn't going to get it with the playoffs starting in April—it was all hands on deck, so to speak.

"Let me get this straight; Mr. Donaldson is hiring us to clean up his image so he can be left alone to prepare for the finals?"

Linda shook her head. "You're half right. We *do* need to give him a fresh look, but he didn't hire us. In fact, he doesn't want anything to do with a PR firm— even if we *are* the best in the business."

Wonderful. Patience didn't mind a challenge, but something told her she was going to regret this assignment long before it was finished. Her Irish-Italian instincts were screaming to leave while she still could. Of course, she didn't listen. "Oo-kay," she said. "Who *is* our benefactor then?"

Linda sidestepped the question by pointing at the player leaving the rink. "Better go down and get the meet and greet over. I have complete faith in you to get this done in the month we've been given." She gathered her satchel from the seat beside her, stuffed the notebook away, and held out her hand. "Do this and we'll have a serious conversation about that partnership, deal?"

Patience contemplated the man, feeling like a voyeur. Now that the practice had ended, his shoulders were slumped and he repeatedly rubbed his temple as he left the ice and disappeared from view. He only thought he had a headache, wait until he heard what she had to say. She sighed and turned to her boss, sealing the deal with a shake. "You owe me a cannoli."

Roy stripped down in the empty locker room and stepped into the shower, sighing as the warm water massaged his back. He'd paid a hefty price to get the arena to himself, but it was worth the fee to escape the merciless eyes of the press. If he wasn't under contract... hell, who was he kidding? His career was all he had left, he wasn't going anywhere. His cell phone jingled, wrecking the quiet. He tipped his head back, letting the water roll off his face. Olivia. *Again.* He had nothing to say to her. She'd made a fool out of him in front of his entire team—unforgivable.

He rubbed his face and blinked unseeingly at the tiled wall. Two months. He and Olivia had been happy together—well, content. God. If he hadn't come home early that day and found her ensconced in his bed...

They'd agreed to take things slow, enjoy the natural growth of their relationship. Instead, she'd stolen his keys, inserting herself into every part of his life. Calling his mother, arranging a dinner with his teammates, adding her name—in a relationship—to his Facebook profile. He pounded the wall, then bowed his head, failure ringing in his ears.

He rinsed off and left the shower stall, hands squeezing the water from his over-long hair—he needed a cut. A startled screech stopped him in his tracks. A curvy brunette sat half-turned on the bench. She'd covered her eyes and held out his towel, reminding him of a pinup from the fifties with her flouncy dress, short sweater and colorful knotted headscarf.

"Who the *hell* are you?" he snarled, making a grab for the towel to cover his privates—though it was probably too late for modesty. So much for having this place to himself.

"Umm, P... Patience Kennedy." She peeked at him from an oversized pair of mint green glasses that made her brown eyes look huge.

Great, they were sending ingénues for reporters now. Didn't matter, he wasn't buying into it. "Well, Patience Kennedy, this is the men's locker room. You aren't supposed to be in here. Tell whatever rag you're working for the whole sex kitten thing is wasted on me." There, that should send her running in...

One.

Two.

The young woman erupted off her seat in the most interesting flurry of bounces and wriggles. Hands on hips, she glared at him in all her bifocaled glory. "That is a horrible, sexist thing to say." Her eyes lowered to his bare chest and the towel tucked haphazardly around his hips. She jerked her gaze up, cheeks flushing a becoming pink. "This is a misunderstanding. My boss suggested I come down and introduce myself after your practice. I wasn't expecting..." Her hands flapped in front of her like a frightened peacock attempting to take flight.

Unexpectedly, he grinned. "Never see a naked man before, Patience Kennedy?" He double-checked the towel and chuckled when she sealed her eyes shut. "Don't worry, your virtue is safe with me." The smile faded. "I learn from my mistakes." He looked around for his clothes, realized he'd left them in his locker and Kennedy stood in his path.

"I wish I could say this has been fun, but..." He waited until she reopened her eyes, then jerked his chin in the direction of the other room.

She tipped her head and a heavy sweep of chestnut

hair slipped over her shoulder to cover the plump full-ness of her breast—not that he was looking. "Sorry?"

He saw the moment the lightbulb went on. Her eyes widened and her mouth made an *oh* that hooked his attention. She had a beauty mark. "My clothes are behind you—unless you plan on holding me hostage until you get your story?" And why the hell did that not sound like a bad idea?

She jumped out of his way and promptly twisted an ankle on the wet bricks. "Ouch," she cried, leaning over to cradle the injury.

That damn sweater was too small, her breasts were hanging out of the top, jiggling with every pained breath she took. He was such a pervert. He crouched to get a closer look at the injury, tucking the towel between his legs. Yep, she'd sprained it. Who came into a locker room in three-inch heels anyway?

"You'd better sit down. You can't walk on it like that." He rose and took her elbow, frowning when she jerked away.

"Don't tell me what I can or can't do. It's fi... fine," she groaned as she put her weight on the foot in ques-tion. Her face paled and she reached behind her for the bench, easing her rump down. "Dammit, what else can go wrong?"

She looked so woebegone; compassion unwill-ingly surged through his chest. He sympathized with anyone going through a rough patch—it was hard not to—but he had no intention of being seduced into doing something he didn't want to do by a pair of big brown eyes. Been there, had the placard.

"Hand me the phone you almost sat on, and I'll call for help," he said.

Patience gasped and lifted her skirt, giving him an eyeful of smooth, milky-skinned thigh before his cell was located. "I'm so sorry," she cried, holding the device to her chest. "Please don't tell anyone about this. You must get injured all the time; don't you have an elastic bandage I could wrap my ankle with? It's not that big of a deal."

Embarrassment flashed like a beacon from her rosy cheeks and dark eyes. Roy guessed she was probably new to her job, looking to make a name for herself as the reporter who landed the juiciest story of the season. He couldn't fault her for that; he was competitive himself. She'd just have to try with someone else—he wasn't interested.

"If I get you the bandage, will you go?" He held out his hand for his phone. He wasn't leaving the room without it.

Reluctantly, she handed the cell over. "I think we got off on the wrong foot, no pun intended. I'm not here to write a story about you, I'm your new public relations representative. I've been hired to help with your image, Mr. Donaldson."

He stared at the disheveled woman in front of him cradling a twisted ankle.

Well, shit.

3

Meraviglioso! Talk about bad first impressions.

Patience hobbled out of the doctor's office an hour later and waited for her ride to arrive. She'd called on her brother and made him promise not to tell Momma, but of course Marco had informed her as soon as he'd dropped Patience off. She'd had to endure a twenty-minute phone call while waiting for the doctor on wearing appropriate clothing when visiting a man.

First, she hadn't been *visiting*, as Momma put it, and second, the lamentable state of her shoe collection wasn't fair. She had a weakness for pretty shoes—didn't everyone? And she did have one pair of sensible sneakers for days off. When she was on the job, she had an image to portray of a successful young businesswoman. How would it have looked to be wearing a nice dress and a pair of grass-stained running shoes? Momma just didn't get it. She'd been a stay-at-home wife and raised her four kids—all boys, except for her baby girl—while Daddy worked his eight-hour shifts at the bakery, and they'd been happy that way.

Patience wanted more from life.

Rush hour traffic made parking a nightmare. Marco had to circle the block twice before he found a place to park so she could get in. After the poking and prodding old Doc Romano had done, her ankle ached. All she wanted was a warm bath and a little vino, not necessarily in that order.

"Thanks for the ride," she said after struggling to climb into his oversized pickup. What was it with men and their trucks, anyway? "And for calling Mom."

Marco just grinned. "At least her focus was on you for a while, instead of harping at me." He signaled and pulled into the slow-moving traffic. "She give you a rough time?" He glanced at her before dropping his window down to allow the carbon monoxide to roll in.

Patience grimaced and turned up the heater. "What do you think? What goes around, comes around, buddy."

Marco sped through a yellow light, causing her to tense and white-knuckle the seatbelt across her chest, before he answered. "I still owe you for that time I snuck out to meet Jenn in high school."

"You're kidding, right? That was forever ago. Hold a grudge much?" Actually, she couldn't blame him for being annoyed. Their parents had grounded him for a month, which happened to include prom night. "Maybe, that's why you became a firefighter, you like climbing through windows."

"Ha, funny girl." He rolled his window back up and turned down the heater. "You sick as well as klutzy?"

Patience glared. She hated the 'K' word. "No. I spent the morning at the Memorial Centre. I might never be warm again." She shivered and pulled her not-so-sensible dress over her knees.

"The skating rink? Taking up a new hobby?" He grinned.

In a family of sports enthusiasts, she was the oddball, and they liked to rub her nose in it. "Yes, Marco. I've been taking secret figure skating lessons for years now and I'm finally ready to go pro. Happy for me?"

He shot her the look. "Sarcasm is not a nice color on you, little sister. Seriously, why the rink?" His eyes narrowed. "Wait a minute... did I hear something about the WarHawks practicing here this week?"

Patience couldn't help it, a picture of Roy

Donaldson in the buff flashed into her mind. Her cheeks heated. She turned her head to look out the side window, avoiding her brother's gaze. A group of three dragon boats appeared just as they were driving over the Bay Street Bridge and she watched, fascinated by the synchronicity of their movements.

"What has Linda got you into this time?"

A few months ago, through no fault of hers, Linda had accepted the client from hell. The woman had been impossible to please, and her husband impossible to avoid. Accusations were hurled, and since she was a local celebrity, it ended up on social media. She'd almost ruined Patience's career, so she understood the consternation in her brother's voice. And prayed to the Lord above that she wasn't making another mistake.

She looked at Marco's worried expression and forced a smile. "How do you feel about season tickets to the WarHawks games?"

Roy SLOUCHED in his seat and traded stares with the team's coach, Charlie Phillips, and the GM. Both men were eyeing him like a slab of meat, and he had a feeling they were less than impressed. Well, so what? He'd been working his tail off; if that wasn't good enough, they could damn well bench him.

"We have no choice, Roy." David Lincoln leaned forward to emphasize his point. "You know as well as I do, the media storm that went down last season after Coach Harris and the doc were arrested hurt the team's image. We can't have rabid fans making it worse." He held up his hand. "Now, just listen a minute. A little PR help isn't going to hurt you while the cops do their thing to catch this woman. Work with us on this, okay?"

Did he have a choice?

Phillips cleared his throat. "I caught the end of practice today. You're off your game. I talked it over with Mr. Lincoln here, and we've decided to give you a couple of weeks to clear your head. Take the time, Donaldson, you need it."

Roy shook his head, stunned. They were starting play-offs soon. He needed all the practice he could get —this was such bullshit.

He shoved his chair back and rose, taking a savage delight in the trepidation filling their eyes. Tempted as he was to smack some heads together, he swallowed the bitter pill. They were upper management; he was just the player.

"You're making a mistake," he said. "If we give in to pressure from the press, they win. Olivia *will* be arrested. I think it's a better spin if I keep my nose to the grindstone instead of leaving town like a... a scaredy-cat from some woman who can't take no for an answer."

Dave Lincoln was already shaking his head and Roy's stomach plunged. "That's the problem right there. You have attitude. It's not winning you any votes with the public, my friend."

Roy's laugh was harsh. "I'm not a bloody politician. Who cares what they think? All that matters is getting my time on the ice so I can perform to the best of my abilities. Christ, this isn't a popularity contest."

"You're wrong," Dave said, moving to wrap an arm around his shoulders and steer him toward the door. "That's exactly what it is. We need the fans to fill those stands. Every year it becomes harder between the cost of tickets and the length of the season. We're walking a fine line here, Donaldson, and we don't need you tipping the scales in the wrong direction."

He opened the door and ushered Roy through. "Take the time. We'll see you in a couple of weeks, after this whole thing blows over, and then we can get down to business, okay?"

Roy gathered his equipment bag from where he'd left it and started down the hall. "It's your funeral, man." He was so pissed he could barely breathe. And it was all because of Olivia. If he got hold of her...

"Oh, yeah," Lincoln called out, "don't forget to pick

up the new PR person on your way out of town. She's going to help turn your image around."

The buxom brunette from this morning filled his head. She could barely speak without tripping over her own cute feet. Roy laughed out loud—this was going to be interesting.

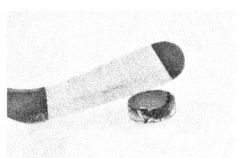

4

P atience stole another look at the withdrawn hockey player. He'd barely said two words since collecting her at her condo bright and way-too-early this morning, but he *had* picked her up a coffee, so she forgave him for that. Not for being a grumpy host though. This was going to be hard enough. If she had to fight his obstinacy for the entire trip, she'd scream.

Not that anyone would hear her out here.

You'd think with three brothers, she'd be used to roughing it, but when it came to household amenities, Patience was a definite girly-girl. Mr. Irritable had informed her they were going to his cabin in the woods *after* they were already on the highway heading out of town. Too late for her to cry sick, darn it.

She stared at the towering trees touching hands

with the sky and felt her world narrow down to the two of them traveling in this ridiculous piece-of-crap-mobile. The dash was faded, the cassette player—cassette player, really?—didn't work, and the windows rolled down manually. Even though she kind of liked the long bench-seat in a turquoise blue, she still couldn't believe this was Donaldson's ride.

"What type of car is this?" she asked in an effort to make conversation more than anything.

He flicked her a glance before lowering the visor against the sun beating in through the humungous windshield. "It's a Cadillac Eldorado—1955. I'm fixing her up."

It was too late for that, going by the rusty fenders she'd noticed earlier. But still, commendable. "I pictured you as more of a rugged truck sort of guy." Like her brothers.

He flicked on the signal light and turned up a steep side road leading straight to nowhere as far as she could tell. "Why? Because I play hockey?" He said it like it left a bad taste in his mouth.

Patience knew, from a conversation with his general manager, that Roy—when had she started thinking of him in first name terms?—wasn't taking the present situation well. And that it fell to her to change his attitude. She wasn't worried about that; she'd had plenty of years to learn how to manipulate her brothers into doing what she wanted. No, it was this insane reaction she seemed to have whenever Roy was near that bothered her. He was handsome, in a dark and dangerous kind of way, but she'd dated good looking men before. Her brothers were always trying to set her up with their friends, and hello, *firefighter*? This was more of a chemical thing. She'd shake it off, she had to.

"Partly," she admitted. "But mostly because it would be sensible since you have a cabin in the back of beyond. Aren't you worried about this thing leaving us stranded out here?" Once again, she looked for signs of life, but unless the trees talked, they were on their own.

His lips quirked. Good to know she was an object of amusement for him.

"I think ol' Bessy will get us there and back just fine. But if she doesn't, we can hike out, it's not that far."

He was kidding right? He had to be joking. She considered walking the half block to the bistro at the end of her street a hike. *Stay strong, Bessy*, she prayed. "You can hike, I'll wait at camp for help to arrive."

He smiled and her insides tingled. "*Stop that*," she warned her misbehaving hormones.

"Stop what?" he asked, his gaze curious.

Crap. She had a bad habit of talking to herself. It didn't matter when she was home in her lonely/quiet condo; out in public, not so much. "Quit watching me instead of the road," she improvised, though it was an increasing concern as the forest closed in around them. "Your precious car wouldn't look so good with a u-shaped bumper."

He laughed. "If I have to be stuck out here for two weeks, at least I'll have entertainment."

Patience's jaw dropped. She wasn't sure what offended her more; being considered entertainment, or not getting asked if she minded staying in nowheresville for *two* freaking weeks! "I can't be away from work that long. Why didn't anyone tell me you were a kidnapper? This is a big mistake. Take me back, Donaldson. Now." She shot him her most serious don't-give-me-your-crap look.

"Sorry, princess, too late. We're here," he said, turning the car into an even narrower overgrown lane.

At least he had to slow down for the winding road. Curiosity temporarily overrode her distress and she leaned forward to see what was around the bend. A burned-out building appeared first, followed by a good-sized log cabin, two stories tall with a wraparound covered deck. Patience sighed her relief. At least they wouldn't have to sleep together. She shushed the butterflies that took wing in her stomach at the mere thought of lying with the hockey player.

"This is... unexpected," she admitted.

Roy pulled up to the house, shut off the car, and

leaned an arm in a black leather jacket along the back of the seat. "Not the shack you thought I was bringing you to, huh?"

His fingers were mere inches from her shoulder and all her nerve endings jumped in response. She turned to rest her back against the door—and put some space between them. "What made you buy a cabin in the woods? You seem a little too career-minded for a getaway like this."

His brows furrowed. He straightened and stared out the window. "I suppose you think I eat, drink, and sleep hockey?" He tapped the steering wheel with nervous energy. "It didn't start out that way." His gaze burned with suppressed emotion. "Look, if we have to put up with each other for the foreseeable future we need to set ground rules. My personal life is out of bounds. You're here to pretty up my professional image, nothing more."

He opened his door and rolled out like a caged jungle cat. "Let's go."

Patience sat, stunned by his attack. The man was complicated. What had she gotten herself into?

5

L ook at them practically making out in the front seat of his car. Olivia tightened her grip on the binoculars and glared a hole in the back of the skank's head. If she thought she was going to step in and take over now that Roy was alone— and missing Olivia—she could forget it.

It had taken months to get close to the burly defenseman before he took notice of her, there was no way Olivia was giving up on them now. They were meant to be together—forever.

"We need to split them apart, then we can take care of *her*," she said, lowering the binoculars to glance at her brother slouched in the passenger seat. "And you're going to help me."

Mike shrugged and lowered the bill of his cap to

cover his eyes. "Whatever. I don't see why you can't just find another suck... boyfriend and let this loser go."

Her brows lowered, but she carefully relaxed her forehead. Momma always said, "Men don't like a woman with wrinkles, so take care of yourself." And Olivia had. Three light meals a day, regular exercises, beauty treatments; it all went toward creating the perfect package any man would desire. But she didn't want just any man, she wanted Roy Donaldson.

"I don't need your advice, Mike. I *need* you to sit up—" she reached over and flicked the annoying cap off his head, "and come up with a solution. You liked Roy well enough when he let you drive his Mustang."

Mike snatched his hat and shoved it over lank blond hair. "It was once, okay? And the car was a '65 original, what's not to like? Doesn't mean I want to help you with this dumb-ass idea of yours."

Unable to help herself, Olivia lifted the spyglasses just as Roy got out of the car and went around to open the door for the chunky woman who climbed out and stared up at the rather impressive log cabin in front of them. What did he even see in her? She had no style sense—seriously, bubble coats when you're plump is like adding wrapping paper to a watermelon, there is no hiding those curves—and what was with those glasses and hairstyle? Did she dream of becoming the next Marilyn Monroe?

Roy put a hand to the woman's elbow and solicitously helped her over the icy gravel drive and up the stairs to the wraparound porch. They paused for a moment while he unlocked the door, then ushered her inside. Olivia's blood boiled. She threw the binoculars onto the seat—where they promptly bounced to the floor—and smacked a gloved hand on the steering wheel.

"She's going to pay for getting in my way," she vowed.

"You're going to jail, is what's going to happen," Mike retorted. "C'mon, sis, you already have a restraining order against you thanks to this guy, isn't that enough?"

Heat rose up her chest and coated her cheeks. "I told you, it's a misunderstanding. Once I get a chance to speak to Roy, he'll clear it up. That's why I need you."

He rolled his eyes. "You're making excuses. He doesn't want anything more to do with you. He's moved on, why can't you?"

Rage rose in a tidal wave. Before she knew what she was doing, Olivia reached down, grabbed the binoculars, and rammed them into her brother's face.

"Ow, you bitch," he yelled, putting both hands up to protect his bleeding nose. "What the hell was that for?"

The anger ebbed, the monster in her head silent for now. She started the truck and backed down the drive until they were out of sight of the house. A couple of maneuvers later, the four-by-four was turned around. Olivia glanced at Mike and frowned. She threw a roll of paper towel from under the seat in his direction. "Clean yourself up, we have a date with a rental agency."

"You're fricking crazy," he mumbled.

She laughed, exhilarated now that the time was near. *Soon we will be together, darling.* And no one was going to stand in her way.

6

Roy opened the cabin door and shepherded the pretty PR woman inside. The scent of pine lingered in the warm air, telling him the cleaning staff had received his message and should have stocked the refrigerator. He'd left everything until last minute in the vain hope Coach would change his mind and take him off of this ridiculous time-out, but instead, he'd been saddled with the prom queen currently primping in front of the hall mirror.

"If you're done beautifying yourself, I'll give you the two-minute tour before I grab our bags."

Patience whirled to face him; her finger held stiffly near her eye. "I'm *not* vamping myself for you," she snapped. "I've been trying to get used to contact lenses, but they're driving me crazy." She dumped the offending lens in a box on the hall table, then reached into her purse and pulled out the geeky green glasses she'd worn when they'd first met. She slid them over her nose and sighed, "That's better."

Her eyes reminded him of a tiger's eye stone he'd had as a kid; shades of brown with striations of mesmerizing gold. Irritated, Roy jerked his chin toward the stairs. "Bedrooms are up there; mine's first on the left, take whichever one you want." He brushed past her and led the way down the hall. "This is the den, help yourself to any of the books in the library." And finished in the kitchen. "The fridge should be stocked. We can take turns cooking—if you know how?" He raised his brow.

She glanced around the well-appointed room. "I think I can manage a meal or two. You have a beautiful home."

He followed her gaze, taking in the quartz counter-tops, the tiled backsplash and high-end appliances. He'd paid a fortune updating the place after... but hadn't spent much time here since.

"What happened out there? I see you had a fire?" She was staring out the window at the charred remains of his garage.

He joined her at the sink, his gut tensing at the disaster. "My buddy stayed here a while ago and ran into some trouble." Roy didn't mention Mac was almost killed, or that their coach was behind the whole incident. The tabloids had a field day then, too. Now, it was his turn. If he didn't believe in creating his own destiny, he'd think his team was jinxed.

"Mac Wanowski, yes, I remember. Your friend is a lucky guy, it could have ended much worse." Patience nudged him with her shoulder. "Making you look good should be a breeze after that fiasco."

Her smile invited him to relax and place his future in her hands, but trust was a precious commodity in his world—it had to be earned. "Yeah, well, about that—" He turned to face her and paused, once again taken by her heart-shaped face and creamy complexion. "Ah, the quicker you do your job, the faster I can get back to mine, so I'm offering a bonus. Do whatever it is you've got to do in a week's time, and I'll give you an extra hundred over and above your fee."

Instead of the gratitude he expected, all Roy received was an eyeroll.

"First, changing an image is not like changing your socks," she said, planting a hand with long, pink nails on her hip. "And second, a hundred dollars is an insult to my abilities. I'm a professional, Mr. Donaldson, I'll do the job when, and how, I see fit."

He had to give her credit, she had spunk. There weren't many men who would stand up to him the way she had. But she needed to learn who was boss.

"Actually," he murmured, strolling across the

kitchen to the back door, "if you want my cooperation, I'd suggest you rethink my proposal. I have every intention of being back on the ice by this time next week." He opened the door and stepped out, the brisk air welcome. "Oh, and by the way, that was a hundred grand—still insulted?" He closed the door on her shocked expression.

PATIENCE PICKED her jaw off the floor and hurried to get a glimpse of the hockey player before he disappeared from sight. He was so... annoying. If they were going to butt heads every time they had a conversation, this was going to be a nightmare assignment. Though she had to admit, the view wasn't bad. He had an athlete's body; long, lean legs, wide shoulders, narrow hips, and an alpha attitude. She was looking forward to knocking him down a peg or two—in the name of enhancing his image, of course.

Her cell phone chirped, startling her. She pulled it out of her coat pocket and smiled at Linda's cryptic text.

Leave the knives at home?

She typed a reply. *You could have warned me. He's a tough client.*

Linda's answer was slow to come. *This is important to me. Do your best, will you?*

Her boss wasn't one to show vulnerability. It threw Patience. *Yes, of course. I won't let you down.* As long as she could get the big bozo onboard.

At least he's easy on the eyes. Wink emoji

I never noticed. Liar, liar.

A clunk on the back deck snagged her attention. *Gotta go, talk soon.* She slid the phone into her pocket and edged toward the door, her throat dry. The city, with all its traffic noise, sirens, congestion, none of it frightened her like that thump on the doorstep. Her brothers would laugh at their chicken-hearted sister.

Gathering up her courage, Patience flung open the door, then shrieked as an orange ball of fur raced past her feet.

7

Roy was still smirking when he rounded the corner of the cabin and strode through the crunchy snow toward his car to unload their bags. The little one-upmanship game he had going with Patience was helping to ease his annoyance with Lincoln and Coach's hard-nosed decision. He understood the economics of the team outranked the wellbeing of an individual player, but it didn't make it any easier to swallow.

He unlocked the trunk and lifted the lid, hefting out the PA's overloaded suitcase. Why did women feel the need to empty their closets for travel? Give a guy a couple of changes and a washing machine and he was good for a month.

He started to lower the trunk lid, but an itch between the shoulder blades made him pause and turn.

If he didn't know better, he'd think someone was watching him. The road leading up here was on private property. If any persistent reporters *had* followed him, he'd sue. Douglas fir, spruce, and the odd cedar stretched to the crisp blue sky and cast long shadows over the ground, sending a chill skittering up his spine. He liked this place for its remote location, but it seemed even a mountain retreat couldn't guarantee privacy.

Shrugging off his misgivings, Roy shut the trunk with a bang, picked up Patience's bag and his own, and headed for the front stairs. It had been drier than normal for January, but precipitation was in the forecast for the next few days, which would likely mean snow for them. First thing in the morning, he'd better chop some wood and get a stockpile for the fireplace. He was curious how the city girl would handle a whiteout.

A scream ripped through the air. Roy dropped the bags and ran, slipping and sliding over the ice, to the rear of the cabin. Patience stood outside, staring at the open doorway, trembling hands over her mouth.

"What happened?" he shouted, his heart hammering. "Are you okay?"

She pointed a shaking finger at the house. "So... something is in there." Her eyes were huge brown orbs against the paleness of her face. "It st... startled me."

Great. A beast was destroying his cabin. "I'm gathering it wasn't a rabbit, then."

A surprised laugh escaped her lips. "Not unless Thumper found a stash of carrots—it was orange."

Orange? That explained her wacky color choices, she must be colorblind. "Well, we know it can't be a bear, they should be hibernating, but it could be a marmot. Wait here until I check it out." Then he remembered the odd feeling he'd had of being watched. "On second thought, you'd better come in or you'll be in the way when whatever it is comes rushing out the door."

That sealed the deal.

Patience practically attached herself to his coattail as they slowly entered the kitchen, scanning every corner for movement. After he made sure the coast was clear, Roy grabbed the broom from the closet so he could sweep the critter out, then made his way to the den with Patience breathing down his neck.

"Do you see anything?" she whispered, her hands throttling his jacket.

"No," he whispered back, then shook his head. She was wearing off on him. "Why don't you check in here and I'll look upstairs," he said in a normal tone of voice. He reached behind and unhooked her fingers. "Here, take this." He handed her the broom handle. "Just pretend you're curling and sweep the animal out if you come across it."

"You're kidding, right?" She frowned, her cute button nose crinkling rather adorably. "What if it attacks?"

If she could only see how fierce she looked...

"Don't worry, its more scared of you than you are of it."

"Famous last words," she muttered as he clicked on the light switch and turned for the stairs.

What was it about Patience Kennedy that made him want to smile? She was like a breath of fresh air in his jaded world. He liked her quirky personality. Maybe, they would make a good team after all. Professionally, of course. He wasn't looking for a love interest. His luck ran o for 2 in that regard.

Though he tried to climb the steps quietly, one of the treads near the top squeaked and he heard an answering skitter from the bathroom situated between his room and the other two bedrooms further along the hall. He glanced over the rail, but all was still, so he continued toward the noise, though his pulse had kicked up a notch. At the last minute, Roy removed his coat, figuring he could use it to either capture the creature or whoosh it out of the house.

The bathroom was dark, the only window facing the trees to the east. Muscles tensed for whatever he was about to find, Roy flicked the switch and held his coat in front of him like a matador.

PATIENCE GRUMBLED under her breath and slowly eased into the den, sweeping the broom from side-to-side in a defensive pattern. He'd left her to fend for herself, what kind of guy did that? If her brothers were here, they'd give him a lesson in conduct—not that she couldn't handle herself, of course she could. She'd learned a long time ago, that men like the ones in her family were few and far between.

Every shadow seemed to move, causing her heart to ricochet around her breast. She remembered a trip they'd taken years ago when a bear had entered a tent not far from their own. The first they'd known of it was when a young woman yelled like a banshee and banged pot lids together scaring the animal away. The experience had ended Patience's innocent pleasure in camping. She felt like that young woman must have felt, afraid and angry, with a healthy dose of wary.

She was halfway through her search of the room when Roy called for her.

"You'd better come see this."

Grasping the broom, as much for comfort as

protection, Patience hurried up the stairs and followed the light to the washroom halfway down the hall.

"Roy?" She crept up to the doorway and peeked into the room, only to see the hockey player down on hands and knees, butt in the air as he looked at something under a beautiful old clawfoot tub.

Curiosity overrode her fear. She edged into the room and crouched beside him, using his back—which was a lot more muscular than she expected, not that she was noticing—for balance. A mangy orange tabby cat stared back at them, tail twitching and copper eyes unblinking.

"A kitty-cat," she exclaimed. "You poor thing. Where did you come from?" She went to pet the feline's head, but a low growl and Roy's quick reaction stopped her from receiving a nasty scratch.

"He's probably feral and maybe even flea-bitten. I'll find a cage and take him to the shelter in town," he murmured, his attention on the animal.

His fingers were warm and sent tingles up her arm from where he held her, so she could be forgiven for not understanding what he'd said. "Oh, good. You can get him food and a litter box while you're there."

He rose to his knees and met her startled gaze. "I'm *not* adopting this cat, Miss Kennedy. I don't have the time or the patience to care for an animal."

She couldn't believe he would be so cruel as to

drop the cat at a shelter and walk away—that was... barbaric. She looked at the frightened tabby and a plan came to mind.

"You have to keep the cat, Roy. This could be the answer to your PR nightmare." She grasped his arm, determined to win him over. "Just think, we can spin the humanitarian angle to the press. The lonely bachelor who saves animals in distress. Your fans will eat it up."

He closed his eyes and took a deep breath before sending her a warning glare. "You win—temporarily. When this thing is over, the cat goes, got it?"

She hid a smile. "Got a name for him?"

"Yeah," he said. "Trouble."

8

Roy rummaged through the storage room in the basement searching for the litter box he'd seen there after Mac had stayed with his black cat, Cleo. Patience had located a few leftover tins of food in the pantry, so he was reasonably sure it was here—somewhere. Funny how fast junk could pile up, and he didn't even live here full-time.

He brushed the dust and cobwebs off the top of a haphazard stack of boxes and read the faint black marker; family photos- 2000. His heart stuttered. He'd forgotten about these old boxes. It had been a long time since he'd gone through them and his hands seemed to work independently to his brain, peeling back the lid on his past and opening wounds he'd thought long buried.

Photos of summers spent here, at the cabin, with

his grandparents and older brother Rick, who'd taught him to love hockey and the outdoors. Ricky introduced him to mechanics and girls and protected him from a sometimes-violent father. Ricky, who had taken his own life and left a confused and angry Roy behind.

Breathing hard, he carefully replaced the cover on the box and closed his eyes. Normally, he could keep the memories tucked away and only pull them out on anniversaries and holidays—this had caught him off-guard. He looked around the cramped room filled with generations worth of odds and ends, everything from Christmas decorations to discarded furniture he couldn't part with after his grandparents passed away and felt like that lost and lonely kid again.

"Roy, are you okay down there?" Patience called down the stairs, her voice anxious.

"Why? Are you going to rescue me if I'm not?" he retorted.

"I can't imagine what that woman sees in you," she snapped and stomped away.

Neither could he. Sarcasm had been his release valve for so many years, it had become a part of him, and more often than not landed him in hot water. Maybe if he'd handled the whole Olivia thing better... too late for recriminations now, all that was left was damage control. He glanced at the wooden beams above him—if he didn't alienate his PA.

The cat box and an open bag of litter sat under the stairs. It would do until tomorrow when he could get into town with a cat he didn't want and a woman who annoyed and tempted him in equal measure.

Patience was nowhere to be found on the first floor, so he left the litter pan in the hall by the door and went out to grab the bags he'd left behind when she screamed. While he'd been in the basement the sun had sunk below the treetops, leaving blue velvet skies. Some people complained about the short winter days in the northern hemisphere, but not him. Nights were mystical; filled with secretive shadows, diamond-studded heavens, glittering snow, and once in a while, the stunning Aurora Borealis. This was, by far, his favorite time of year.

Filling his lungs with invigorating night air, Roy hoisted the bags and hefted them up the steps. Inside, the low murmur of a woman's voice drew him to the second floor and the room Patience had commandeered. He lifted his hand to knock on the partially open door but paused when he heard his name.

"Don't worry about Roy, he comes across as a hard case but he's really a pussycat on the inside."

A pussycat, huh? There were many names he'd been called over the years, but a pushover wasn't one of them.

He pushed the door open and entered the room

with her bag in tow. The cat—Trouble—laid his ears back, hissed, and jumped off the bed he'd been lounging on to duck underneath. Patience was sprawled on her tummy and looked at him over her shoulder. "You scared him," she chastised.

Roy took his time dragging his gaze over shapely legs and an apple-shaped bottom in form-fitting jeans, before he finally landed on her raised brows. "Keep that thing off my bed," he said, setting her suitcase near the dresser.

Patience rolled over and came up in a rush, her ample breasts doing interesting things under her pink sweater. "This *isn't* your bed, at least not while I'm here."

His lips quirked; her cheeks reflected the color of her shirt. She talked tough but he had a feeling she wasn't nearly as assured as she pretended.

"Yes, ma'am," he said. "I brought your bag up. Anything else you need before I turn in for the night?"

She slid off the bed and rose, straightening her clothes. "Already? It's kind of early, isn't it?"

He grinned openly now. "Why? Are you scared of the bogey man?"

She frowned, her eyes crinkling rather adorably at the corners. "I was hoping we could get started on a plan for your new image."

The reminder of why she was here wiped the smile

from his lips. "That's your job, Ms. Kennedy. I'm just tagging along for the ride."

Her eyes sparked at his words. She poked a finger into his chest. "Look, we have to work together, or this will never succeed. I realize you couldn't care less about anything other than hockey, but this gig is important to me and I need you to cooperate, *capisci?*" She poked him again.

Damn, she was cute when she got mad.

He grabbed her finger, stopping it from digging a hole in his chest. "Point taken. Tell you what, give me time to have a shower and I'll meet you downstairs. Are you any good at making hot cocoa?"

She stared at him, bemused. "Sure. You haven't had hot chocolate until you try it Italian style."

He took a stray strand of soft brown hair and slid it behind her ear. "Sounds like you know what you're doing," he murmured, his heart kicking up a beat when she licked her lips.

"Oh, I do," Patience answered, peering at him through thick, dark lashes. "That's why your general manager hired me."

He blinked, his brain slowly clearing from the sensual fog they'd created between them. "You're a cool one, Patience Kennedy. What would it take to break that veneer, I wonder?"

He shook his head at his own stupidity and walked out the door.

PATIENCE RELEASED a gusty sigh the instant the door closed behind the too-tempting hockey player's lean backside. He'd made her feel like a firecracker about to blow its top and he hadn't even put any effort into it —*whew*.

Linda had a strict rule against fraternizing with their clients, one that Patience had never come close to breaking until now. Her brothers would heartily approve of Roy; a man's man, the type of guy you could count on to save the world—just don't ask him to share his feelings. Like Ken. Her ex could never understand why she needed to *talk* out their differences. He was much more willing to skip ahead to the make-up sex part of the arguments.

The cat slunk out from under the bed and sat looking at her, his head tipped.

"At least you're willing to listen to me, aren't you, Toulouse?" She tried out the name from one of her favorite books as a child.

He turned his back on her and paced to the door. "Meow."

"So, I guess you aren't bilingual then," Patience

said with a chuckle. "Okay, let's go see about dinner, buddy." She straightened the messed-up covers on the bed, opened the door, and followed the tabby down the hall, hesitating for an instant in front of the closed bathroom door. The low rush of the shower and the fresh citrus scent of body wash seeping into the hall brought disturbing visions of the first time she'd met Roy storming into her mind. Muscular, tanned. Wet. Skin.

Pulse pounding, she hurried away before he caught her gawking—his ego was big enough without her help.

The night was oppressive behind the kitchen windows, so Patience pulled the blinds and got busy with the promised hot chocolate. She located milk in the refrigerator, poured a tiny amount into a bowl, and whisked in a bit of corn starch before setting it aside. Next came cocoa and sugar in another bowl, then it was time to heat the milk. Nice, he had a beautiful gas stove. She wondered if he liked to cook or if his girl-friends were nominated for the chore. Once the milk boiled, she lowered the heat and whisked in the corn starch mixture and dry ingredients, then added thick chocolate pieces she'd found in the fridge along with a touch of cinnamon.

The cat twined around her legs purring.

"Smells good, doesn't it?" Patience agreed, stirring the slowly thickening drink until it took on a rich, shiny texture. She turned off the stove and moved the pot to the back burner for safety, then bent to pet the cat. "Your turn, now. How about tuna surprise?" The purring increased, suggesting he liked the idea. "Feral, my butt," she muttered.

"What's that about your ass... ets?" Roy said.

Startled, Patience glanced up and froze. Roy leaned casually against the doorframe, his hair slicked back, brown eyes—a match for her hot chocolate—crinkled at the corners and lips quirked. A ribbed gray sweater and dark jeans highlighted his physique and left her at a loss for words.

"Cat got your tongue?" he teased, entering the room to pop a spare piece of chocolate lying on the counter into his mouth.

"My tongue is fine, thank you," she retorted. "I was just telling Toulouse here that he's a true gentleman."

Roy raised a skeptical eyebrow. "What kind of name is that? I like Trouble, it suits him." He stepped closer and stirred the cocoa. "This looks interesting."

Affronted, Patience rose too fast and bumped her head on Roy's outstretched arm. The pot wobbled on the burner and would have tipped if he hadn't grabbed the handle with his other hand, effectively trapping her against the stove.

"Sorry—"

"You should come with a warning label," he said overtop her apology.

Now, she really was sorry—that she hadn't bumped his face. "Are you always so... so miserable?"

He stared at her mouth. "You have something..." He touched her upper lip, "there."

Embarrassed, she licked at the spot, tasting chocolate. "I had to sample my recipe. It's good, by the way." The heat from his body was like an inferno, that's why her cheeks were on fire—had to be.

"Tempting," he murmured, leaning closer.

Holy Hannah. He was going to kiss her, and she was going to let him. Her body readied for the moment their lips touched, eyes closing, chin raising, heart stopping. And then...

"Yeow," Roy cried, jumping backward as the cat released its claws from his leg. "That damn cat just attacked me."

Bemused, Patience looked from Roy rubbing his calf to Trouble/Toulouse sitting at her feet innocently cleaning his paw.

She burst out laughing.

9

Roy sat across the table from Patience sipping surprisingly tasty hot chocolate and wondered how he could feel so... well, relaxed, when his career was basically imploding. "What did you put in this drink? It's addictive."

She apparently took that as a sign he needed more, rising to bring the pot over to fill their cups. "It's proven that chocolate contains the chemical phenylethylamine which releases endorphins to make us feel good. Is it any wonder it's the number one choice for Valentine gifts?"

"I'll have to keep that in mind," he murmured, entranced by the gorgeous mahogany-brown fall of her hair as she leaned forward to refill his mug. She was lovely in the way of silver screen movie stars, luscious and soft with an underlying fierceness he secretly admired. He had a feeling she could handle whatever came her way—he envied her strength.

"Sorry," she said, resuming her seat. "My brothers and I played a lot of Trivial Pursuit as kids and I like to win."

He caught the present tense and smiled at her not-so-subtle warning. "That's something we have in common... winning," he clarified at her questioning glance. "So, tell me about these brothers of yours. Should I be worried?"

"Are you an arsonist or a bank robber?" She tipped her head quizzically. "No? You should be safe then." She sipped the cocoa, then wrapped her hands around the mug. "Seriously, I have three brothers—all over-achievers. Marco, the oldest is a firefighter. Paul, named after my father, is a police detective. And Franco just received his paramedic certification. Then there's me, the baby in the family." She pushed her drink aside and pulled a laptop over. "We should get to work—if you're ready?"

"Yeah, sure," he said, watching as she opened the computer and deftly clicked at the keyboard. Obviously, he'd been wrong. The tough woman he'd pictured had a few chinks in her armor, after all.

She turned the computer so he could see the screen

and slid her chair closer. "I suggest a three-pronged approach; interviews on all the major stations, a few charity events, and a public apology."

He'd been with her until the last one. "What do I have to apologize for? It's not my fault some crazy broad won't take no for an answer." Now he knew how women felt when men came on too strong—angry and helpless.

Patience raised a brow at his temper. "Attitudes like that won't do you any favors. The idea is to put a positive spin on a shitty situation. An apology would go a long way toward appeasing your fans." She sighed. "Look, just think it over, okay? We can start with the interviews and go from there."

Roy pushed away from the table and paced the short length of the kitchen; back and forth, back and forth, like a caged tiger. He felt as ornery as one, too. "This is ridiculous. I didn't do anything other than end a disastrous relationship, and for that I've been hung out to dry. All I want is my life back. Is that too much to ask?"

"Of course not," Patience replied. "But, unfortunately it's a sad fact that supposedly wronged women will be believed without question. The #MeToo movement might have done a lot to bring women's rights to the forefront of public conscience, but it also created a guilty until proven innocent mentality. It's our job to showcase the person you truly are and knock out the media storm that's been following you since your girlfriend's exhibition."

"Ex," he snapped. "Ex-girlfriend." Where was a skating rink when he needed one? "This whole thing is turning into a gong-show." Filled with restless energy, he opened a cupboard door, then slammed it shut, startling the cat who jumped, all four feet in the air, then scrambled across the floor and disappeared around the corner.

Patience pursed those full lips of hers and gestured for him to take a seat. "About the interviews, I can set it up so most are done remotely, meaning Skype or phone-in radio talk shows. But I think it's for the best if you agree to at least one or two television meetings." She raised a hand when he opened his mouth to protest. "I know, you value your privacy and resent the hell out of me, your boss, the entire world right now. But, trust me, I *will* make this right for you—as long as you level with me, okay?"

What choice did he have? It was either this or kiss his career goodbye, and that was something he refused to give up without a fight.

He stared at Patience, testing her mettle, but she only raised her chin and met his gaze. Wanting, needing the last word, he kicked back in his chair, lifting the front two legs off the floor, and smirked while inside his guts twisted into knots. "Give it your best shot, Kennedy. I'm counting on you to score with this one."

10

Two days later...

Patience pushed her notepad across the table and tapped on the large black print, *Expand your Answers.* Roy answered by using her paper as a coaster, setting his sweating water bottle squarely in the center of her recommendation. If the radio newscaster was half as frustrated by his one syllable sentences as she was...

"It's such an honor to have Roy Donaldson, winner of last year's James Norris Memorial Trophy and defenseman for the Victoria WarHawks with us today. Before the break, we opened the phone lines and I see many of you have questions, so we'll get right to it. Hello, you're on KPLY Sportsdesk. Please tell us your name and what you would like to say to Mr. Donaldson," the announcer, a veteran reporter, intoned in a bored voice.

Patience knew where he was coming from. Roy was making almost no effort at all. He had stoic down to a fine art. Frustrated, she kicked his leg under the table. Darn man, he brought out her orneriness. He flinched and shot her a glare over the open laptop just as the first caller came on the line.

"Ted Freemont here. Hey, Samson, I was at the game in Vancouver when Wanowski pulled that hat trick—great game. It's not fair what they did to you, man. Will you be back before playoffs?"

Roy mouthed a curse and straightened in his seat. Patience held her breath and prepared for damage control.

"Yeah, Ted, thanks for the support. The Hammer really took it home that game. We're working on a solution, but between you and me, nothing's going to keep me away from my team come playoff time. Leave your name and info at the station and I'll make sure you get some skybox tickets for a home game, sound good?"

"Wow, man, yeah, thank you. I tell all my buddies you're the best, Samson, even if you did that crap to your girlfriend."

Oops, and it was going so well, too. Patience swiveled the laptop around before Roy could react. "Thanks, Ted. Roy is taking a short break, folks. See you in five." She waited for the *clear* text to come through, then sent a swift reply to the station before closing the lid on the computer. "So, that was awkward."

Roy folded his arms and stared her down. "Want to explain what he was talking about? What *crap*?"

Damn. She should have told him sooner, but he'd been different out here, less stressed. She hadn't wanted to ruin it and hoped the whole thing would blow over, frankly. Guess not. She took off her glasses on the pretext of giving them a good cleaning. "A couple of days ago, just after we arrived, your girlfriend made an announcement—ex," she hurried to correct, flicking him a glance beneath her lashes. Yep, definitely, not a happy camper.

His teeth ground together audibly. "What kind of *announcement*, Kennedy?"

He used her last name like a curse. Was it wrong she found it kind of hot? "Umm, well, Olivia did an interview with the *Times Colonist* and declared she's pregnant—with your child. She says that's the real reason you dumped her and that when she told you about it you threatened her if she didn't get an abortion."

It wasn't true, of course it wasn't. Still... Patience slid her glasses back on and his grim face came into sharp focus. "Did you know she was pregnant, Roy?"

His fists slammed down on the table, upsetting the water bottle. "Seriously? Is that what you think? That I would turn away a woman in need? One carrying my child—which is bullshit, by the way. I use protection. Every. Time." He rose and clenched his hands on the back of his chair. "She's going to ruin me, isn't she? How am I supposed to beat this?"

The bleakness in his eyes cut her heart to ribbons. He'd just taken a body slam and it was her fault. She could have, should have, prepared him for this setback. What kind of personal assistant left their client to wander around in the dark? It was her duty to ferret out anything detrimental to his image and counter it before it could gain traction. She'd failed.

And that pissed her off.

"Okay—" she said, righting his water bottle and rising to meet him eye to chest, "new plan. We're going to change tactics. Instead of ignoring the problem, you're going to face it head on. What do you call it? A face-off. Yeah," she lifted a finger and shook it, "a face-off. She's the opposing team and you're going to do what you do best—beat her at her own game."

His brows had slowly risen at her outburst and now those firm lips quirked. "Whoa, remind me not to get on your bad side—you're a tiger in disguise, Patience Kennedy."

Heat suffused her cheeks. "I'm sorry, Roy. I let you

down. If you want to fire me, I totally understand." She refused to lower her chin, though it was the hardest thing she'd ever done.

Roy shook his head and moved around the table to grasp said chin. The pad of his thumb feathered her lower lip before coming to rest along her jawline. Her silly heart performed cartwheels at the intimacy. She froze, everything within her leaning into the touch, and waited. Wanted. Anticipated.

"I'm not letting you go just yet," he murmured. "We have a contract."

His words had the undesired effect of cooling her ardor. He was right, they had a contract. And if she wanted to keep her career, she'd better remember that.

Just then, her cell phone buzzed from its spot on the table, saving her an awkward retreat. She took a step back, figuratively and literally, and turned the screen so she could read the text: *thirty seconds to airtime.*

"It's the station, they're ready for you." She kept her gaze down, opening the computer and dragging it out of sleep-mode. Sadly enough, she could see similarities between herself and the machine. Time for both of them to wake up.

"Patience..." Roy looked at her with something like regret. "I didn't mean to suggest anything."

Could her face get any hotter? "I know. Could we

get down to business, please? My advice is to shoot straight from the hip. If someone asks you about... you know, Olivia, tell them the truth. Diplomatically, of course," she hastened to add.

He hesitated, then nodded and resumed his seat. "Sure, if that's what you really want." He looked at her meaningfully before turning to the computer. "Let's get this over with."

Feeling like she'd lost something precious, Patience keyed in a response to the waiting announcer: *We're ready*.

"And we're back with WarHawks defenseman Roy Donaldson. Roy, are you ready for your next caller?"

Roy locked eyes with Patience. "Bring it on, Sam."

"Great. Caller number two, you're live on KPLY Sportsdesk. What would you like to ask our hockey hero today?"

There was a brief spurt of static, then a woman's voice came through, sharp as cut glass. "I want to ask my fiancé when he plans to quit running like a scared chickenshit and step up to the blueline—the one on my pregnancy test, that is."

Patience's eyes widened even as Roy's expression turned arctic cold.

Olivia.

11

Blood rushed through Olivia's veins, pounding in her ears and at her temples, as she waited with bated breath for Roy's response. She'd been planning this virtual meeting ever since the radio station started advertising word of the upcoming interview with the *great Roy Donaldson.* Each time they clashed it reminded her of the thrill of being with him. She'd never had a lover like Roy, and she wasn't ready to give him up to some overblown bimbo. He belonged to her.

"Hello, Roy? Are you still there?" she sing-songed, getting a kick out of poking the bear.

"I'm here," he answered, his voice a controlled growl *almost* better than foreplay. "Why are you doing this, Olivia?"

Because you're worth it, popped unbidden into her

head, along with the hurt. She was grateful for the tide of anger that flowed behind it, killing the pain the way he'd destroyed their relationship. The way she was going to ruin him.

"Why, honey, I don't know what you mean. I realize becoming a father is a big step, but I didn't expect you to run the other way." She smirked, practically seeing the steam coming through air waves.

"Don't turn this on me. I broke up with you because you're crazy and not for any other reason. I am *not* your baby's father, so you can just take this stupid game you're playing and shove it up your..." His voice became muffled as though his mouth was covered. A moment later, *she* came on the air.

"I'm sorry, Mr. Donaldson isn't feeling well—a flu bug. He would like to thank his listeners and assure them he will be back to work in no time."

The announcer's voice was overloud in the spartan hotel room. "Well, of course. Sorry we had to cut the interview short, folks, but that's the way it goes in showbiz." He gave an awkward laugh. "Any final words, caller number two, before we return to our regular programming?"

The old coot. He wanted a sensational story to spike his ratings. Just so happens Olivia had one to share.

She set her voice to shaky. "I didn't mean to cause a

scene. Roy and I, we've been through tough times. He has a temper—not that he'd ever hit me—he's not like that, but... sometimes... Anyway, we'll work it out. Call me, Roy. Soon." Satisfaction flared. Other than the touch of venom at the end, she'd hit the right notes of heartbreak and hope. No one was going to stand behind him now, least of all his damn teammates. He'd be blackballed for life. Lost and lonely. Just the way he'd left her.

Once again fury took over and Olivia flung the burner phone across the room, shattering the mirror over the cheap dresser. She stared at her reflection in the splintered glass, emotions as fractured as her image. Angry tears rolled down her cheeks and her hair looked as though she hadn't brushed it in a week. She was falling apart, and it was all that damn hockey player's fault. If obsession was a sickness, then she was dying.

It had to stop.

She scrubbed trembling fingers through her hair, wincing at the knots, and turned as the door opened and her no-good brother stepped through the entry, bag of groceries in hand.

He took one look at the damage she'd done and turned to leave. "Looks like you're busy," he mumbled.

Impatience met dark humor. He was an idiot. "Get in here, you imbecile. You can help me clean this mess up. I can't afford another room."

Obviously reluctant, he closed the door and set the bag on the wobbly table in front of ugly brown drapes closed for privacy. "We'll be lucky if we don't get kicked out. Geez, sis, what happened?"

She shot him a glare. "It was an accident, okay? Just help me clean it up, and for Pete's sake, don't cut yourself. I can't stand the sight of blood." Though she might make an exception if it was Roy's.

"Not to mention me bleeding to death," Mike grumbled, but he got down and began piling the pieces into the waste can.

Olivia left him to it, closing herself in the utilitarian bathroom. She needed a shower. It was time to up her game.

12

Roy couldn't remember the last time he'd felt this helpless. That... that woman was making a laughingstock out of him. He didn't even want to contemplate if she'd been telling the truth. It was bad enough imagining he'd be tied to her for life, but his child...

God, what a mess.

"Are you okay?" Patience stood on the other side of the table twisting her hands, forehead furrowed, big brown eyes dark with worry.

Much as he wanted to vent his dread on her unsuspecting head, he couldn't. Olivia was his mistake, not hers. "I'll live," he said. "Not so sure about her though."

Patience's eyes widened. "You don't mean that—do you?"

Don't tempt me. "So, Miss Brainwave, any other great ideas? The interview was a wash."

"You can't give up at the first setback. Where's your competitive spirit?" Patience pulled the notepad close and brushed at the water stain before giving up and flipping the paper over. She looked at Roy and raised a brow. "Come on, what would your coach say?"

He couldn't help it, he grinned. "Nothing your delicate ears should hear," he admitted. Sighing, he pulled up a chair and nodded toward the notebook. "Not sure a playbook is going to help us against this nemesis—she's not afraid to break the rules."

Well," she said, "in my eyes Olivia just gave away her game plan. I say we stick to our original strategy and prove to your fans you aren't the person she's trying to paint you as."

"What if I am?" Roy stared past her, unwilling to see the disillusionment in her gaze. "What if she's telling the truth and there really is a baby?" He turned to her, his gut roiling.

Patience reached out and grasped his hand. "Then you'll handle it," she said, squeezing his fingers.

Would he? Roy wasn't so sure. When his brother had needed him most, he'd let him down.

He sat back, deliberately breaking the connection between them, and crossed his arms, fingers tingling from her touch. "I'm glad you think so, let's hope we don't have to find out." He lifted his chin toward her notepad. "What's next, boss?"

Patience hesitated, then looked down at her list. "I have you booked on *The Morning Show*, *Ellen*, *Jimmy Kimmel* on Monday and *Canada AM* the next morning. I didn't want to reach out to too many until I knew how you handled it. This should give us a good foundation to go by."

"Whoa," he said, holding his hands up. "Does *Ellen* even watch hockey?"

Patience smiled. "She might after she meets you —*if* you turn on that charm I've read about and win her over."

No wonder she was so good at her job, she could sell snow to an Eskimo. "I suppose next you're going to tell me I need Instagram and Twitter accounts."

"Great idea," she agreed and promptly lifted her cell phone. "Smile."

Roy blinked against the brightness of the flash. "Hey, what was that for?" His phone dinged and he pulled it from his pocket to see an incoming text from... *Patience*. He looked at her and raised a brow.

"Just open it," she said, giggling.

He stared a moment longer, captivated by the humorous slant of her lips and the twinkle in her expressive eyes. Patience Kennedy was pretty in a sweet, sexy way that appealed to him more than he liked or wanted. Once burned, twice shy.

He tapped in the passcode and opened his phone to retrieve her message—it was the picture she'd taken of him with Trouble hovering in the background. "I already know what I look like, but thanks." Dour and uncompromising, like his father. Shrugging the ugly memories away, he turned to search for the cat. He sat near the back door, watching them with unblinking gold eyes. "I think your cat wants out."

"Oh no, you don't," she said, rising to pick up the big tom and cuddle him to her chest—lucky cat. "Your house, your cat. My condo doesn't allow pets."

He gazed at her skeptically. "Whatever you say," he murmured. He'd take the feline to the pound tomorrow after their trip to the vet. There was no room in his life for anything but hockey. Then Patience bent to set the cat down, revealing the curving plumpness of full breasts above the cut of her shirt, and his pulse stuttered.

He cleared his throat and quickly returned his attention to his cell phone. "I assume you had a reason for this?" He waved the instrument in the air.

She snagged it out of his hand quicker than any wingman. "If you're going on Instagram you need a photo to share," she said as though he should know.

"Your @handle on the team is Samson, right?" He nodded and she tap-tapped for a few more seconds, then handed the phone back. "There you go. Ooh, look, you already have ten likes."

Roy stared at her in bemusement. "What am I supposed to do now?" He didn't do social media, had no interest in the cutthroat world of popularity polls.

"It's easy. Take a picture, add a few hashtags, and you're done. Even you can handle Instagram, Donaldson." She smiled encouragingly, and he snapped a photo. "Hey," she said. "I didn't mean me."

He followed her previous directions and the next thing he knew likes and comments were flooding the feed. "Look, I did it."

Patience leaned over his shoulder and read the comments aloud while he tried to ignore the tantalizing scent of her hair that reminded him of sunshine and lavender.

"Who's the new woman in @Samson's life?"

"I guess we know what he's doing instead of playing hockey."

"Wonder what Olivia thinks?"

Roy turned his head at the last one and his mouth grazed Patience's oh-so-soft cheek. She gasped and froze, and he forgot what he'd been about to say. Slowly, so as not to frighten her away, he lifted his arm and cupped her face, applying enough pressure to line their lips together. She moaned low in her throat and the kiss ignited, teeth scraping, tongue twisting, passions flaring. He traced the column of her throat, the rapid beat of her pulse sending a sweet shot of triumph through his extremities.

His phone dropped with a dull clunk as he reached around and tugged her onto his lap. She stared at him with a hunger that twisted his gut. A faint warning whispered in his mind; he was messing with a woman who technically worked for him, never a good idea. He ignored it to wrap her arms around his neck and nibble the delicate skin of her jawline. Patience's head fell back, granting him access to her throat, the rise of her breasts, the feel of her sweetly rounded butt in his hands. He was in so much tro...

Trouble.

The damn cat leaped onto the table, scrambled across and jumped off the other side, startling them apart. Patience laughed nervously and hopped off his lap like a scalded... well, cat, leaving him with a raging hard-on and nowhere to go. He had to try though, grasping her hand before she could get far. "You don't have to leave," he rasped and had the satisfaction of seeing her shudder.

"Roy, we can't. My job..." She tugged free and clasped her arms around her waist. "I shouldn't have kissed you like that, I'm sorry."

She was sorry? He was the idiot getting hooked on another woman when he should know better. Time to get his head in the game. "Don't worry about it, just passing the time, right?" He rose and headed for the door. "I'm going to bring more wood in, don't wait up."

13

The trip to town the next morning was made mostly in silence. The only one willing to vocalize his displeasure was Thomas—he seemed to like that name better than Toulouse—who was periodically yowling from the box Roy had closed him into.

Patience glanced into the backseat for the tenth time, partly to check on their passenger's condition, but mostly to gauge the other male's disposition. He didn't look any happier than the cat.

"So, tell me about the cabin. You said your grand-parents owned it?" she prodded, determined to get a conversation out of the sourpuss.

Roy effortlessly steered the tank he called a car around a snowdrift and flicked on the wipers against the sleet that had started halfway down the mountain.

"My brother and I couldn't wait for summer vacations. Gramps took us hiking and fishing, and Grandma filled us up on her legendary baking—it was the best."

The affection in his voice as he spoke painted a vivid picture of a happy time in his childhood. "Are they...?"

He nodded. "It's been a while now. They went within a year of each other. It was hard to return to the mountain, at first, but I'm coming to grips with it now— they wouldn't want me dwelling on the past."

"And your brother? What does he do?" She was filled with an insatiable curiosity about all things Roy Donaldson.

He jerked the wheel and Patience's shoulder slammed painfully against the door. He pulled to the side of the road and parked, breathing heavily.

She slowly straightened, rubbing her arm. "Umm, was it something I said?"

He sent her a dark look, colder than the freezing rain bashing the car. "No. Yes. I don't want to talk about it."

Message received. Though she couldn't help but think maybe he should speak to someone—not her, obviously—over his repressed feelings. It might be another reason why he had trouble committing to a relationship. The little bit she'd seen and heard of Olivia made her wonder how much of the problem was hers and how much was a lack of communication with the man currently glaring out the window like *The Hulk* before he did his big reveal.

Come to think of it, *The Hulk* had anger management issues, as well. Maybe he could recommend a good therapist to Roy. She smiled at the thought of Roy laid out on a couch while a psychiatrist tried to get him to share his *feelings*. Good luck with that.

"What's so funny?" he muttered, raking a hand through wavy hair the color of autumn leaves.

"I was just picturing you as a superhero," she said candidly, then flushed at his raised brows. "Not that I think you are or anything," she sputtered. "It was a random thought, forget it."

Now that she was the one flustered, his good humor returned—funny how that worked.

"Well, darlin', I can be whatever you want me to be," he murmured, resting a beefy arm along the back of the seat.

Patience grimaced and edged away from the temptation of those fingers so near her shoulder. If he touched her again like he had last night, she'd go up in smoke. "Why do you do that? Whenever there's something serious to discuss, you deflect." She waited for the teasing light to die from his eyes. "You can talk to me, Roy. I hope you know that."

He took his arm—and the promised warmth of his

touch away—and shifted the car into gear. "You pulling double-duty there, Miss Kennedy? PA and MD? What's next, the GM?"

It took her a moment to figure out what he was getting at, but when she did, she gasped and socked him in the arm.

"Hey," he said, jerking the wheel again. "Don't hit the driver."

"Don't accuse me of narcing out to your boss, then. That's not the way I do things. If there's something I need to talk over with your general manager, you'll know about it, *capisci?*"

"Are you always this touchy?" he asked. "Your brothers must have driven you nuts as a kid."

She stared out the windshield, the countryside changing from the white blanket of snow to green moss and giant ferns as they dropped into the Comox Valley. He was right. Being the only girl in the family, she'd often felt left out and had learned to bully her way into her brothers' lives. Her mixed Irish, Italian heritage didn't help either. Two more hotheaded cultures would be tough to find.

"My brothers were all athletic. They won ribbons every year at school fitness competitions, played basketball and hockey. Their friends were jocks, too. As you can probably tell—" Patience swept a hand down her curvy body, "I wasn't. It made me defensive, even though they were always nice to me." The ocean peeked in between the buildings huddling closer and closer as they neared the center of town. "I used to dream of being the prettiest, most popular girl in school. The one all the boys wanted to date, and all the girls wanted to be—silly, huh?"

"Not silly at all," Roy murmured, pulling into an empty parking spot in front of the veterinarian's office. "I can't believe you weren't that girl."

Startled, she turned, sure he was mocking her. Instead, he stared at her with appreciation and something that looked a lot like attraction. Flustered, she jerked her gaze to the box on the backseat. "I hope Thomas doesn't hate us too much for bringing him here."

Roy shrugged, opening his door to climb out of the car. "He'll be even more unhappy when I drop him at the pound afterward."

What? He was kidding, right? Thomas was *not* going to the pound. Over her dead body.

Or Roy's.

She jumped out and stomped around to his side of the car just as he lifted the box from the back. An orange paw poked through one of the air holes, then disappeared inside. "See, he just gave you a big fat finger for that. You can't give him away, it's bad luck."

Roy chuckled and closed the door. "I wouldn't be

surprised if he did communicate his opinion of me. In case you haven't noticed, that cat hates me. He'll be better off with a family who can give him the attention he deserves." He waved for her to lead the way onto the sidewalk. "C'mon, Trouble, let's get you fixed up."

Patience opened the vet's door and followed Roy in, the scents of antiseptic and dog making her nose wrinkle. A boxer sat up when they entered, and his owner tightened his grip on the leather leash in his hand. A gray and white cat sprawled across the reception counter, the king of all he surveyed. Thomas growled and the container rattled in Roy's arms.

A young woman popped up from behind the counter, her cheeks turning rosy the moment she caught sight of Roy. "Oh, hi," she said. "I was just looking for our resident hamster. He escaped his cage—again." She laughed and glanced at the box. "Do you have an appointment?"

Roy rested the carton on the counter. "Yes. This is Troub... Thomas." He grimaced when Patience elbowed his ribs. "He's a stray, so I'd like him to have a complete checkup and get him neutered at the same time."

The receptionist smiled, obviously bowled over by the sheer charisma of the hockey player. "Do I know you from somewhere?" she asked, her brow furrowing rather adorably. "You look so familiar."

Patience stepped up, aware Roy hated his notoriety at the moment. "Can we get Thomas out of this box? He's not used to being confined." To punctuate her words, the cat kicked up a sudden fuss, howling and hissing and relaying his displeasure at the situation. The gray and white cat jumped up like he'd been scalded and leaped from the counter when the boxer barked.

The receptionist got the message and hurried toward an exam room. "Right this way, please. The doctor will be with you shortly."

She closed them into a small room with a steel table, a closed cupboard, and a shelf with gloves and other medical tools. Roy set the box on the table and carefully opened the lid. Patience held her breath, hoping Thomas would behave like a gentleman.

All was still for the count of five, and then, as though it was a walk in the park, the cat hopped out of the crate and gave them a baleful look before lifting a leg and proceeding to clean himself.

"Don't you wish you were that agile?" Roy murmured.

Patience looked to see his trademark smirk in action, and she burst out laughing.

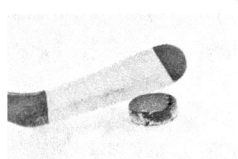

14

Guilt dogged Roy's steps as he and Patience left the vet's office and strolled down the street. When the doctor picked up Trouble to take him into the operating theatre, he'd been tempted to grab the poor critter and make a run for it. Neutering might be the responsible thing to do, but as a guy... Ouch.

"That was tough," Patience said, as though she'd read his mind. "Thomas wasn't happy."

"Trouble, not that it matters since he's going to the pound later." Double the insult—poor cat.

"Let's talk this out on a full stomach, I'm starving." Patience nodded toward a diner down the street. "How about there?"

Roy wasn't a fan of public places, but he couldn't very well say no to her request, so he nodded and placed a hand on her back to guide her across the road. She stiffened at his touch, then sort of leaned into his hold. It felt like they were a couple. Probably looked that way, too, but he couldn't make himself care. She... fit. If someone wanted to snap a photo and spread it around social media, let them. He almost wished they would; it might push the Olivia debacle into yesterday's news.

"Oh, good. They serve all-day breakfast." Patience smiled up at him, filling his chest with a warm glow.

They entered the busy little restaurant and a cheerful middle-aged server guided them to a table overlooking a marina. Boats of all shapes and sizes floated on gently lapping waves. He'd often thought of buying a sailboat and drifting down the Pacific coast, maybe even to Mexico, but had never found the time to take the lessons—though that could change if he didn't get back to the ice soon.

"Peaceful, isn't it?" Patience interrupted his musings. Her gaze was soft as she stared out the window. "My dad had a boat while we were growing up. Nothing like these," she admitted with a smile, the dimple in her cheek flirting with him. "Just a canoe, but we loved taking it out on the water. It changes a person's perspective—lets them see the world from a different point of view." She straightened in her seat as though embarrassed she'd revealed such a personal memory. "Kind of like we're trying to accomplish for you. I meant to tell you; I received a text from my boss. She heard your interview and she liked it, Roy." She reached out and squeezed his hand, eyes shining. "The preliminary reports show public support is climbing in your favor. It's like I said, Olivia overplayed her hand."

Roy leaned back and allowed the server who'd swept in with a pot of aromatic coffee to fill their cups and hand them menus. After she moved on to the next customers, he tapped his fingers on the table, oddly unsure he wanted to ask the question burning a hole in his gut.

"What is it?" Patience tipped her head and looked at him quizzically. "It looks like the cat got *your* tongue." She smiled, clearly enjoying a chance to return the pun.

"Does this mean I can go back to work?" Funny, he'd been waiting to hear those very words, but now... not so much.

Her enthusiasm dimmed and he was sorry to douse the fire. "No, I'm sorry. We're committed to the television guest spots I booked for you, and besides, your general manager wants to get to the bottom of the baby scandal before he'll let you *lace up*—his words, not mine."

The pressure in his stomach eased, though he refused to admit it was relief. "Fine," was all he said, lifting the menu to make a wall between them. They'd only known each other a scant few days, but Patience Kennedy was already leaving an indelible mark on his heart.

"Are you mad at me?" she asked, using a slim finger with a pink-tipped nail to lower his menu so she could meet his gaze.

He gave up avoiding her and dropped the menu onto the table. "No, it's not your fault. I just wish I knew what Olivia was up to, that's all." He took an appreciative sip of coffee and let his eyes wander the diner. Couples and families occupied most of the seats. A large group of seniors packed a table along one wall and he could see their server laughing and teasing them as she took their orders. A lone woman sat at a two-seater at the front of the building, her chair facing the street where they'd come in. Something about... A couple stood and chatted with the young family at the next table and when they moved, the woman was gone. He turned toward the till, but only the pair were there, paying for their bill.

He shrugged and turned back to Patience. "Have you decided what you want?" The more time he spent in her company, the more he knew what he wanted, and it didn't involve food.

Olivia had foolishly stormed out of the hotel room without her purse, so she was stuck wandering the streets of this boring little town with practically no cash in her pocket. She could have returned and taken the keys to the truck, but it was a matter of pride. Her brother had always known what buttons to push and she hated him for it. Unfortunately, she needed help and Mike was the only one she could trust. Which meant she would let him live—for now.

Storefronts threw up sickeningly sweet displays of hearts and flowers, cupids and chocolate as though the whole world couldn't wait to celebrate Valentines, the day of love.

Love.

If there was a more fickle emotion... She'd learned at the hands of a pedophile father who'd promised love even as he did things that would have put him in jail if she'd told. But eight-year-old Olivia had already learned the value of twisting the truth to get what she wanted. He'd paid for her silence, she made sure of it.

Cold, she entered the next business she came to, which happened to be a coffee shop. The server led her to a table for two, as though she knew without asking that Olivia was alone.

"Get me a coffee," she said, dismissing the woman with a flick of her hand.

"Why yes, your majesty," the frump said, strolling away with the speed of a snail.

Olivia frowned at the server's rudeness, then shrugged, turning her chair until her back faced the restaurant. It bothered her to see families enjoying themselves, maybe because hers never had. Her mother had died when she was six. After that it was her, Mike, and their father. She still remembered the elation she'd felt when he'd been killed in a freak accident on the job. And then there were two.

"Your coffee. Can I get you anything else?" The server looked down her nose and waited.

"Hmm? No, that's all. Thank you," Olivia added, wrapping cold fingers around the ceramic mug.

Nonplussed, the waitress nodded. "Just shout if you change your mind. But not *too* loud." She smiled and left Olivia alone.

She sipped her coffee and tried to ignore the ache blooming in her chest. Kindness was a rarity in her world, it was the reason she'd fallen so hard for Roy. He'd treated her with respect—at least until she'd borrowed his keys. To be fair, he shouldn't have left them where anyone could take them. She'd been seeing herself out after a wonderful night of hot-as-sin sex and there they were, sitting on the bureau, gleaming in the moonlight. It had started out as a joke, her sneaking in to leave cute notes, or a piece of sexy lingerie to tempt and tease. But then it graduated to something darker—compulsive. When he quit calling, she went through his drawers, sure he must be seeing someone else. She accessed his computer—predictably, he'd used the team as his password—and trolled his emails, anything that would hint at his state of mind.

When Roy accused her of taking his keys, she'd denied it, but he'd told her they were over and changed his locks, effectively cutting her from his life. Or so he thought.

A couple crossed the street down the block, the man's hand guiding the woman safely onto the sidewalk. It was only when he glanced toward the restaurant that Olivia realized it was Roy. *Shit*. She wasn't ready for a confrontation yet. It had to be on her terms, and without that bitch as a witness.

Crap, they were coming in. She sank down on her chair and held the cup in front of her face, desperately hoping he wouldn't look into the window. He didn't, but her relief was short-lived. His gravelly voice coming from behind her seat sent shivers coursing down her spine. She watched as the server—her server—led them to a table on the other side of the café, but not far enough that she couldn't spy on them through the window's reflection. He looked good, dammit. She stared holes in the woman he was with, hoping she'd choke on her food and expire right there because no one knew the Heimlich maneuver.

Of course, nothing went the way she wanted. They spent the next hour ignoring the crowd swarming in and out of the busy diner. The smiles, the little touches, the looks, it was too much. Olivia started to rise, then froze when Roy's gaze panned the restaurant and landed on her. Did he recognize her? Did he feel the animosity rolling in his direction like a black cloud? Maybe, now was the time. Her hand tightened around the bread knife from her place setting. Once, through the heart, that's all it would take. The woman would die, and Roy would come home begging on his hands and knees.

Just as she turned to attack, a young couple stopped at the table behind hers and chattered like magpies with a family with two children—a boy and a shy young girl. It froze Olivia in her tracks. She was bombarded by memories of happier days, before her mother passed away. Days when she still believed in unicorns and rainbows and happily-ever-afters.

Biting her lip against a heart-wrenching sob, she dropped money from her pocket—a twenty—on the table to pay for her coffee and hurried out of the café before she once again made a fool of herself.

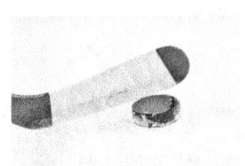

15

Patience wandered in and out of the local stores, conscious of Roy trailing behind, doing his best not to attract attention. It was funny, on the ice he was larger than life, but take him out of his comfort zone and... he became a man. An incredibly handsome, slightly vulnerable man.

"What are you looking for?" he asked, as they entered yet another shop—this one a pharmacy.

She held out a carmine and white plush bear holding a heart with the words *Be Mine* embroidered into the fabric. "For my brother."

"The fireman?" Roy's lips quirked. "I'm sure he'll love it."

She returned the plushy to the shelf, tempted to keep it for herself. "I think I'll stick to chocolate, it's a safe bet."

Roy pointed out a pair of red velvet handcuffs. "I'll take a set of those," he joked, a mischievous twinkle lighting his eyes.

Patience smirked. "Is that the only way you can hold onto a woman, Donaldson?" Then she realized what she'd said and clasped a hand over her mouth. "I'm sorry," she mumbled. "That came out wrong."

The lightness of the moment evaporated, but he took pity on her, tapping a flushed cheek. "Trust me, sweetheart, if I used them on you, you'd beg me to throw away the key." He turned and wandered down another aisle, leaving her staring after him, hot and flustered.

Holy Hannah, the man packed a punch. Suddenly, she could see what drove that woman to chase after him like a lovesick fool. She reached out to touch the cuffs, then hurried after Roy before she did something stupid—like testing his theory.

A few minutes later they were back on the street with nowhere to go.

"Did the vet mention how long Thomas's umm... procedure would take?" she asked, back to being uncomfortable in his company.

"They'll call when he starts to come out of his anesthetic."

Lovely. If she was alone, she could easily use up the time at a library or bookstore, but Roy didn't look the studious type. Maybe they could split up and do their own...

"Hey, look. They have a public skating rink here." Roy strode over to have a better look at the poster plastered to the wall outside the pharmacy. "We should go. You skate, don't you?"

"Of course," she said. "Three brothers, remember?" *Just not very well.* Maybe if she held onto the boards...

"Great. You can show me what you've got, Kennedy." He grinned.

"Yeah, sure." Like how many times she could bounce when her feet went out from under her. As they walked the few blocks to the Recreation Centre, Patience tried to come up with a believable way to avoid the humiliation she was about to endure. "I should prepare your dialogue for Monday. Why don't you go ahead and I'll just—"

Roy clasped her hand and dragged her along with him. "Oh, no you don't. I've had to dance to your tune for the last few days, it's my turn. We're going to have some fun for an hour and forget about Olivia, hockey, your boss, everything. You with me?"

How could she say no? He deserved a break from the stress he'd been under. And truthfully, she wanted a chance to see him in his environment. "Lead on, but you should know I kinda, sort of embellished my skating prowess."

He raised his brows. "You fibbed? I'm shocked." He chuckled at her wounded expression. "C'mon, it's never too late to learn. You might be a natural."

Not likely. The last time she was on the ice—a *long* time ago—she'd made a fool out of herself trying to show off for a handsome senior in her school and ended up in the hospital nursing a broken arm. Fun times.

The building was predictably large, a gray brick monstrosity with a fitness room, swimming pool, concession stand, and ice arena. The air was moist and filled with chattering voices from the families coming and going. It was fairly busy, and Patience had the fleeting hope there was a class in session, but the rink was open—oh, joy.

Suddenly, it dawned on her, "Skates. We have no skates, darn it. I guess we'll have to try another day." Or not.

A man in dark blue coveralls straightened from watching the kids on the ice. "There's rentals available at the concession booth, back the way you came."

"Got it, thanks," Roy told the guy and turned to her. "Wait here, I'll go. What size?"

"Umm, nine?" Great. Now he knew she had big feet, too. Nothing delicate about Patience Kennedy. She sighed.

"Is that...?" The caretaker lifted his cap and scratched his head as he watched Roy walk away.

"Nah, it can't be." He turned to Patience, a curious look on his grizzled face. "Not from around here, are ya? I know most everyone in this town, been here my whole life."

Patience smiled, relieved he'd let Roy's identity slide. "No. We're from the city. My... friend's family own a house up the mountain, we're staying there for a few days." She carefully stepped across the rubberized flooring to a nearby bench and sank down to remove her shoes. "Hope I don't embarrass him," she muttered.

The caretaker took the handle of a broom that had been resting against the wall and pushed at some non-existent dirt. "I saw the way he looked at you, miss. I don't think that's what he's feeling."

He winked and carried on with his work, leaving Patience with her jaw hanging open. He'd intimated Roy was, well, interested in her. They had a chemistry she couldn't deny—her stomach fluttered just thinking about his kisses—but that's all it was, attraction. He'd been through a bad relationship and she had her career, it could never work.

"Ready to get your feet wet?" Roy asked, holding up a pair of worn hockey skates, and in that moment, she knew it was too late—she was already going down for the third time.

Roy finished tying his skates and stood, eager to get out on the ice. After months at practice camp and then competing in hockey games since the season began, the last few days had felt like he was back in ninth grade playing hooky so he could hang out with his brother. Funny how it was the times they'd gotten into trouble that gave him the most bittersweet memories now.

"Ouch," Patience grumbled, sucking on her finger.

Roy's gaze narrowed on the distracting sight. With those red lips and wind-tossed wavy hair, it was all too easy to picture her in his bed. And since that thought was guaranteed to make crouching to help her a challenge, he cleared his throat and channeled his inner grumpy old man. "What did you do now?"

"Humph," she muttered, showing him the wet skin of her finger and a slice alongside the nail. "Those dam... I mean darn—" A couple of boys passed by, pushing and shoving each other as best friends do, "—skates bit me."

She looked so insulted he had to chuckle. "I'm pretty sure that's not possible. Let me see." He carefully took her hand and examined the wound. "I think you'll live. The bleeding has mostly stopped, but I can ask around for a first aid kit if it would make you feel better."

She tugged free and hid her hand in her lap. "No, no, that's fine, but I won't be able to do up my skates now, so I guess I'll watch while you have all the fun." She smiled innocently.

He had to give her points for effort. She really must be terrified to get on the ice. It just made him more determined to teach her that it wasn't as bad as she figured. "No worries, I can do up your skates." He bent down and wrapped a hand around a shapely calf. "Give me your foot, princess, and I'll try on your glass slipper." Their gazes met and he read the mixture of embarrassment and awareness in hers, recognizing it as a reflection of his own emotions. "You can trust me. I won't let you fall." For him or the ice—she was bound to get hurt either way.

"Are you trying to convince me you're Prince Charming?" Patience slid her foot into the skate he held open and rested her hand on his shoulder for balance as he tightened the laces.

The trust implied in her touch did weird things to his chest. "I'm no one's hero." He yanked on the ties to finish and gain some space between them. He'd quit caring what people thought the day his brother took his life. He rose and took a step away. "There, you're set. I'm just going to take a quick tour around the rink. See you out there?"

Hurt flashed in her pretty brown eyes before she caught herself, forcing an unconcerned smile. "Yeah, sure. I'll be the one hugging the boards."

Guilt rode his shoulders, competing with the pure exhilaration of stepping foot on the ice. In just a few strides he was up to full speed, gliding around the edge of the rink as though on rails. The cold air brought tears to his eyes, obscuring the people out for a casual skate stopping to stare as he roared past. He was causing a spectacle, but the taste of freedom felt so good he was reluctant to let it come to an end. Then he caught a glimpse of Patience and skidded to a stop, a fan of ice spraying out behind him. *Who the hell was she talking to?*

As he drew closer, she reached out and drew a tall, dark-haired guy into her arms, kissing his cheek. She hadn't mentioned a boyfriend. Roy's hackles rose. He'd kissed her and she hadn't said a thing, dammit.

Patience saw him coming and let the guy go, but not before she patted his broad chest. Rather than looking uncomfortable, she smiled when she saw him. "Roy, I want you to meet my brother, Paul. He says it's a coincidence but I'm pretty sure Mama sent him to check up on me."

Roy held out his hand in greeting, the band of tension in his gut easing. "The cop, right?"

Paul gave him a piercing stare from ice-blue eyes—startling with that dark hair. "Police detective, actually. I was in the area and thought I'd stop by to see my little sister."

Read, check if he'd done anything to her. "I'm sure she's happy you're here. How *did* you know where we were, by the way?"

"Yes, *Paul*, tell Roy what you've been up to," Patience said, grasping her brother's arm for balance. Was it wrong that Roy wanted to be the one she looked to for safety?

Paul shrugged, obviously not fazed by his sister's betrayal. "I heard she had a new client—you—and looked into your background. The report said you have a stalker problem, so I asked some guys on the force here in town to keep an eye on my baby sister. No big deal."

Except that he'd invaded Roy's privacy. "You ever hear of a thing called the Privacy Act?" he muttered.

Paul bristled and it would have been fairly impressive if he wasn't six inches shorter than Roy and lean rather than wide in the shoulders. Didn't stop the guy from getting in his face though. "You got something to hide, Donaldson?"

Patience gasped. "Paul. What is the matter with you? Back off. I don't need you checking up on my clients like that. Jeez." She pushed him away, promptly lost her balance, and would have fallen if both men hadn't made a grab for her—Paul snagging her wrists and Roy her waist. Miffed, she slapped their hands away and stumble-glided to the wall where she worked her way to the entrance. "Men," she snapped and awkwardly stepped off the ice to disappear from view.

Roy stared after her, bemused, then turned to her brother. "What did we do?"

Paul grinned and slapped him on the back. "Welcome to the family, man."

16

P atience wobbled to the nearest ladies' room and collapsed on a wooden bench. Her legs hurt only marginally less than her feet and she hadn't even accomplished any ice-time. The person who'd invented skates must have done it as a form of torture. She fought with the knots Donaldson had tied in her laces, flinching when she accidentally caught her sore finger in one of the hooks.

She couldn't believe Paul had shown up out of nowhere like that. Or that he'd been investigating Roy. She loved her brothers, but they drove her crazy with their overprotective attitudes. *Didn't they realize it's the twenty-first century? Women's lib is a thing!* And Roy—she thought they'd connected today. She'd been having a really good time with him and assumed he was too, and then he'd pulled the moody male thing and left her to make her own way onto the ice—which had been his darn idea to begin with. *Ooh, men.*

A blonde with classically beautiful features exited one of the stalls and paused as though shocked to see anyone in the room. Patience offered a friendly smile just as her phone jingled in her coat pocket. She pulled it out and read her boss's name on the display.

"Linda, I was just thinking about giving you a call." She felt the other woman's gaze on her and turned away for privacy. "Did you get the memo I sent?"

"You mean the one about the interview that's trending all over social media?" Linda said. "What happened, Patience? It's your job to make sure the crazies don't get between you and your client. You failed, big time. Maybe I should take over this one before—"

"No!" Patience glanced over and met the stranger's eyes in the mirror over a lineup of utilitarian sinks. She shivered at the cold stare and lowered her voice. "No, I have everything under control, really. Don't worry, I know what's at stake."

"Do you? Because from where I'm standing, you're heading for a train wreck. One that could adversely affect my business. I can't let that happen, not even for you."

Patience didn't know what to say. It almost sounded as though... "Are you *firing* me?" Her stomach dropped to her pinched toes. She kicked the skates off, her body trembling at the thought of losing the career she'd worked so hard to build.

"Of course not." Linda sighed. "I only wanted to remind you how important this assignment is, that's all. Roy Donaldson is a media icon. The eyes of the country are watching. If he looks bad, so do we."

Patience frowned. "And what about the witch who won't leave him alone? Why does she get away scot-free? All Roy wants is his life back, is that so bad?"

The bathroom door slammed back on its hinges, startling her into almost dropping the phone. She twisted in time to see the blonde shoot a furious glare her way before stomping out of the room. How strange. Maybe she was PMSing. The thought made her smile, relieving some of the tension from the phone conversation.

"I'm sorry, Linda. I messed up; it won't happen again. Trust me, I'm invested in clearing Roy's name as much as he is. I have a partnership on the line—that is if it's still an option?"

"Honey, I'm not that cold-hearted. I'm sorry if I came across too firm. Consider this a warning; check and double-check your itinerary with Mr. Donaldson. We can't afford any more mistakes."

"I will. And thank you," Patience said before ending the call. What a mess. She needed to focus on her job and put the attraction she felt for Roy behind her. At the end of her contract with the hockey player they would part ways and she'd never see him again. She had to keep that in mind.

Heart heavy, she rose and prepared to leave, then gasped at the obscene letters scrawled in blood-red lipstick on the mirror—BITCH.

ROY SHOOK his head and started to follow Patience off the ice, but her nosy brother grasped his arm.

"Hold up, would ya? I have a few questions, and I'd rather do it while my sister is out of the way." Paul's buddy-buddy smile faded and the intimidating expression that probably made him an ace police detective made an appearance.

Roy understood. If Patience were his sister, he'd feel the same. But he still wasn't going to allow this guy to run roughshod over him. "If you're looking for a good restaurant, I can recommend the diner in town, otherwise I can't help you, Detective."

Paul's poker face held firm. "I read the police report you filed against one Olivia Brandt. She's a resourceful young woman. I have to ask, Donaldson, is my sister safe with you?"

How was he supposed to answer that? Because he

had a feeling it wasn't just the cop asking, it was a worried brother. A family skated nearby, the mother helping her daughter take her first steps while an older brother shouted encouragement from the sidelines. Yes, he understood the protective love of a sibling.

"I can't make any promises," Roy admitted. "But I would never do anything to deliberately hurt Patience. What Olivia would do if she considered her a threat, I can't say. She hasn't done anything physically to me—so far—but she loves to play mind games. That's why your sister is here. My GM hired her to clean up the mess Olivia has made of my career. Truthfully, I don't think there's much Patience can do, but I'm willing to try."

"So, you two aren't...?" Paul frowned.

Heat rolled up Roy's chest to his face. He rubbed the back of his neck and chuckled, though he'd never felt less like laughing. "Hell, no. I just got rid of a crazy girlfriend, I'm not in the market for another."

"What is that supposed to mean?" Paul bristled, then forcibly relaxed when the family gave them a nervous look. "My sister may be, well, eccentric, but she's not an idiot. You'd be lucky to have her—don't tell her I said that."

Roy could see Patience's quirky humor in her brother. "I think your sister is..." He stumbled over the right description. Funny. Sexy. Beautiful. None of those would endear him with Paul. "... great, but we're both focused on our careers. This is a professional relationship, nothing more." Great speech; too bad he wasn't sure who he was trying to convince, Paul or himself.

"I have to head back to the city today. How long are you planning to keep her out in the boonies? Italians are close-knit, we like our families nearby. Ma's already making noise about Patience being gone." Paul skated toward the exit.

Roy took a last regretful glance around the rink, sorry he had to leave, then followed the detective. "I have a few television interviews coming up on Monday, so we'll be back to the city by then. Your sister didn't waste any time with her plan of action."

Paul grinned over his shoulder. "She's a powerhouse, that one. Three older brothers and she bossed all of us around from the time she was in diapers."

Roy sympathized with them. He'd met her barely a week ago and already she had him jumping through hoops. *Women.*

There was no sign of Patience. Maybe she had gone to the concession to grab them a coffee. He smirked. The way she'd left the ice, he'd be lucky if he didn't *wear* the coffee.

He removed his skates and pointed toward the

bathroom as he stepped into his shoes. "Mind watching for your sister while I'm gone?"

Paul looked up from untying his laces. "Yeah, sure. I want to say goodbye to her before I leave, anyway."

Roy nodded and strode into the spacious restroom, sidestepping a wet floor sign. The caretaker they'd run into earlier looked up from filling the mop pail at a utility sink.

"You and your lady have a good skate?" he asked, turning off the water.

"She's not... used to skating but managed well." Roy couldn't bring himself to write off their non-relationship. It was bad enough he'd lied to her brother—because there was definitely something going on between him and the PA, and it wasn't all business.

The man dumped some liquid into the pail and the scent of bleach filled the air. "I watched your last game," he murmured, squeezing the mop out and slapping it onto the cracked and pitted cement floor. "Wasn't right what that woman did to you, just wanted you to know you have people on your side." He looked up and away, as though not sure he should have said anything.

Roy swallowed hard around the lump forming in his throat. Through this whole experience he'd held his peace—other than filing the restraining order—unwilling to slander Olivia's character, though she hadn't suffered the same restraint. It was a relief to hear not everyone thought he was a slime ball. "Thanks," he said, striding over to grasp the man's hand. "It means a lot."

The caretaker's grip was strong. "It's a real pleasure to watch you play, Mr. Donaldson. A real pleasure."

"Roy, please." Roy reached into his pocket and pulled out a business card. "Next time you're in the city, give me a call and I'll get you tickets to a game."

The man stared at the card like it was gold. "Wow, thank you. Never been to a live game—well other than the kid's tournaments."

Ah, he was a hockey dad. Roy remembered his own mother and father ferrying him back and forth to early morning practices, sometimes on ice-laden roads. Hockey parents deserved awards. "Does your son still play?"

"He's a coach. The kids love him." Pride shone from his crinkled eyes.

Roy nodded. "Well, it's people like you and your son that helped give me my career, so I owe you." He smiled and turned toward the urinals. "Guess I better hurry up or my friend is going to wonder if I got lost."

"She seems real nice. Best of luck to you both," the man said, pushing the pail across the floor. "See you around, Mr. Donaldson." He pushed the pail to the end stall and started to wash the floors.

Roy expected to see Patience sitting with her brother by the time he left the restroom, but he was alone. "Still no sign of her?"

Paul rose and frowned. "Women take forever in the bathroom, but this is ridiculous. Maybe I should get someone to check on her."

"I'll ask the caretaker, I just saw him." Roy started toward the men's room just as Patience burst from the restroom, her face ashen.

She glanced wildly up and down the long hallway, stopping when she noticed him on the other side of the corridor. "She was here, Roy. She was right here."

17

Patience huddled inside Roy's coat and cradled the cup of coffee he'd brought over, her nerves frayed. He'd raced outside the arena in search of Olivia, but she'd vanished. If not for the crude message she'd left behind, they would never have known how close she'd been.

Paul stood deep in conversation with a couple of Mounties near the propped-open door to the women's restroom while Roy was taken to a nearby office to be questioned by the investigators and Patience had been warned not to go anywhere—as if she would.

A crowd had gathered on the other side of the yellow tape, cell phones out, recording every nuance of the scene. Patience felt too fragile to deal with them and turned toward the now empty ice rink. She'd been grilled on the woman's description, mannerisms, comments, anything and everything until she'd thought her head would explode. Underlying all of it was the question of why she hadn't realized she was face-to-face with Olivia Brandt. In her defence she'd never met Roy's nemesis and photographs didn't do her justice. The woman could be a model with her svelte frame and chiseled cheekbones. She'd colored her hair to ash-blond instead of brunette, but it was her brazenness in showing her face mere feet away from Roy and violating the judge's ruling that had the investigators concerned. That and the threatening message.

Paul sank down and nudged her with his shoulder. "How you doing, kid?"

"Other than feeling like an idiot, you mean?" She rested her aching head on his arm. "If I'd only realized sooner..."

"You can't blame yourself. I'm just glad you weren't hurt. When I think what could have happened —" He shuddered. "Donaldson has a lot to answer for."

Patience jerked upright, and inwardly groaned as black spots floated in front of her eyes. Tension headaches were the worst. "It's *not* Roy's fault and don't you dare blame him. How was he supposed to know his girlfriend is crazy as a loon?"

"Girlfriend, huh? What are you doing with him then, and I don't mean your job, either?" Paul glared right back.

"Ex, Paul. She's his ex-girlfriend. Not that it matters. Roy and I are... friends." She took a sip of the cold coffee, her gaze going to the still-closed door of the office. They were taking a long time. Roy must be so frustrated. "What's going on in there?" she muttered.

"Not enough, considering my baby sister was just threatened. You're coming home with me," Paul growled.

"Don't be ridiculous," she snapped. "I'm a grown woman, Paul Kennedy. I make my own decisions, whether you like it or not." She rose as the office door *finally* opened and Roy appeared, his expression grim.

"Were you always this stubborn?" her brother said, joining her. "He doesn't look impressed."

They waited while Roy shook the officer's hand, listened to some final words, and made his way over to them, ducking under the yellow tape.

He ignored Paul to rest a gentle hand under her jaw, tipping her face up for his inspection. "Are you okay?"

His concern when she'd expected anger brought tears to her eyes. "I'm fine," she whispered. "I'm so sorry, Roy. If I'd paid more attention—"

"You might have been injured," he finished. "I knew she had issues, but this... this is scary. I think you should go back with your brother. It's too dangerous for you to be near me. Olivia has gone over the edge."

"See?" her brother crowed. "I just said the same thing."

Patience broke free of Roy's hold and took a step away from both overbearing men. "Do you forget I have a contract to fulfil? Your general manager hired me. You don't have the right to stop me from doing my job—either one of you." She'd worry herself sick if she left Roy to handle Olivia on his own.

Roy shook his head. "I've already put a call through to Lincoln. As soon as he gets back to me, you're off the payroll. I'm sorry, but I can't risk you getting hurt."

He'd gone behind her back. How was she supposed to recover from this? Linda would be upset. It might even cost her the partnership, though it wasn't her fault. And Roy. How was she going to forget him?

"What about my clothes? And Thomas?" she pleaded. "We're so close to clearing your name, please, don't send me away."

Paul frowned. "Are you begging?" he asked incredulously. "And who the heck is Thomas?" He turned to Roy, hands clenched. "What have you done to my sister?"

"You're causing a scene," Patience hissed, lifting her chin toward the avid crowd. "He didn't *do* anything to me, get your mind out of the gutter. Thomas is a stray cat, Paul. Not part of a threesome orgy—*jeez*. It's lovely to know what you truly think of my character, brother."

Paul cringed but didn't back down while Roy stared on with growing amusement. "An orgy, huh? Why didn't I think of that?"

Patience turned beet-red. She pushed up her glasses on a suddenly sweaty nose and tried to ignore the sparks going off under her skin from the electricity in his gaze. Images of satin sheets and bare skin bombarded her senses, making it hard to think.

"You know what I mean," she muttered. "This is stupid. We overreacted and once again played into Olivia's hand." She looked meaningfully toward the crowd, busy on their cell phones. "How long do you think it's going to take before this story goes viral? It's what she wants, Roy—to ruin your reputation."

"And if it's more than that?" Paul asked, as usual, the voice of reason. "We—the police force—can't ignore a direct threat such as Miss Brandt made today. Until she's under arrest, it would be best if you distance yourself from the situation. You'd only be in the way of our investigation and use up valuable resources for protection details."

Paul's words had hit home. She was losing. She could see the regret in Roy's eyes. They barely knew each other, really, but the thought of never seeing him again created a heavy weight on her chest. She wasn't ready to say goodbye—to him or to Thomas.

Thomas.

"You're not going to take the cat to the pound, are you?" She grasped Roy's arm. "You can't, he's ours now." They'd rescued the animal together, maybe they could share custody? "I'll ask my superintendent. She might be lenient if Thomas only stays with me part-time."

"And I suppose you want me to keep him the rest of the time?" Roy raised his brow. "I told you that cat was trouble." His gaze softened. "No guarantees, but we can give it a try, okay?"

Patience couldn't control the joyous smile that spread across her lips. She and the hockey player were the proud new parents of a cantankerous ginger cat. She didn't have to give them up yet.

"See you Monday?" she asked, anticipation curling like smoke through her veins.

"Are we still doing the interviews then?" He glanced at Paul. "Will that work?"

Paul's gaze went from Roy to Patience, settling on her flushed face. "I guess if saving your heinie from the press is that important to my sister we'll have to figure out a way to make it happen. Don't expect much alone-time though," he warned. "We'll be keeping a close eye on you."

Embarrassment warred with relief. It didn't matter, she had a reprieve.

"See you Monday," Roy murmured and defied Paul to brush a kiss across her cheek. He nodded at her brother and strode away, the crowd parting and then swallowing him from view.

"I hope you know what you're doing," Paul said, his gaze worried.

Living, she wanted to say. When Roy was near her pulse thrummed. Her skin seemed sensitized, anticipating the moment they might touch. He made her feel like a bottle of expensive champagne; buoyant.

"I have no idea," she admitted. "But I have to try."

Paul gave her a rare hug. "I hope he's worth it or else I'll kick his ass."

Touched, she squeezed him back and closed her eyes to pray Roy didn't break her heart.

18

Roy sat on a swivel chair in front of a mirror in a crowded dressing room. He tried not to fidget while a hair stylist messed with his hair and a makeup artist dabbed his brow with a puff ball. Every once in a while, a long-drawn out whine from Trouble, holed up in a cat carrier, echoed his sentiments; what the hell were they doing here?

Because Patience promised she would be here.

Somehow, in the past week his priorities had switched from getting back on the ice—though he missed the team—to his headstrong, quirky, beautiful PA. Maybe when the hype was over and his life got back on track, he'd ask her out for dinner.

A date.

He hadn't taken a woman out on a date since high school. He wasn't proud of it, but the notoriety that came with being a professional hockey player meant women approached him. Casual hookups were easy— no emotion necessary. Even with Olivia, though she'd held on longer than most. Maybe because she'd done all the work in their relationship. She'd show up at his car when he was done with practice, a smile on her pouty lips and wine in hand. Sometimes they'd make it back to her place before sex, but not always. He should have picked up on the desperation sooner, but instead had accepted what she'd offered without thought to her feelings. For his part, she gave him a welcome relief from the stress of his job. For her... an unhealthy obsession.

Roy's phone rang and his heart jumped. But instead of Patience, it was Coach. He gave the two attendants a meaningful stare. They blushed and set down their equipment—obviously, according to the cluttered table, it was hard work making him look good —and hurried from the room.

"Is this my call-back?" he asked, placing the cell on speaker so as not to smudge his makeup—not a problem he'd ever thought to have.

"More like a call-waiting," Charlie said. "As in waiting for you to do something constructive so you can get your butt back here where it belongs. We need you, man."

Roy stared at the caricature of himself in the

mirror. Not that the stylists weren't good, it's just that he was sick and tired of jumping through hoops when all he wanted was to play hockey. After this season, he would be a free agent. If the WarHawks didn't want him, he'd find a team that did.

"What do you want from me, Coach? I'm doing every damn thing the PA *you* hired has asked me to do and apparently, it's still not good enough. Either put me back in the lineup or I'm done." His hands clenched on the arms of the chair. Either he'd just jumpstarted his career or signed its death warrant.

"You know I can't do that until the GM gives the go ahead. Look, we have another two weeks before the team goes up against the Canucks. If we beat them, we seal ourselves a spot in the semi-finals. Think you can make Lincoln happy before then?"

The only thing that would make the general manager happy was if he were to suddenly become married with two-point-five kids and a white picket fence. Roy had a feeling the guy had been a Bible thumper in another life.

He stood and carried the phone over to the cat crate, bending to get a look at Trouble. Sleeping. He was recovering from the surgery but wasn't thrilled with the world at the moment. Roy sympathized, he wasn't feeling the love, either.

"I'll do the interviews already lined up. After that

it's up to you." He hung up on the coach and tossed the phone on the couch. The cat woke up and stared at him with golden eyes. "I know, I went a little hard on him, but what choice do I have? I'm going stir-crazy sitting around like this."

He stretched a couple of fingers into the cage and rubbed the tom between the ears, half-expecting the sharp crunch of teeth breaking through his skin. Instead, a low rumble started like a classic sports car idling at the start line. "Where's your momma, huh? She's supposed to be taking care of us. I don't know about you, Thomas—don't tell her she won—but cameras scare the heck out of me."

"I won what?" Patience asked.

Roy jumped, then promptly let out a curse as his fingers caught in the wires of the cage. The cat hissed and glared at him as if it was his fault the carrier almost hit the floor. He righted the enclosure, then turned and... stared.

Patience stood just inside the doorway, backlit from the hall lighting, looking for all the world like an angel dropped down from Heaven. She wore a white eyelet dress with a scooped neckline and a pencil skirt that damn near stopped his heart.

"Roy?" She took a couple steps closer on a pair of heels that could be designated as deadly weapons.

"How's Thomas?" she asked, catching sight of the carrier.

He moved aside so she could check on the animal—and he could enjoy the view as she bent over the cage. Sue him, he was a guy. She glanced up and raised a brow, and he belatedly realized he'd yet to say a word.

"He's, uhm, fine." He cleared his throat and waved a hand at her getup. "What's with the fancy clothes?"

She made sure the cat had settled, then straightened. "I wanted to portray a businesswoman image—too much?"

Not for the business he wanted to have with her. He moved the half-step that brought him toe-to-toe with the most fascinating woman he'd ever met. She was a mess of contradictions with those librarian's glasses, intelligent eyes, and voluptuous body.

He leaned in and gently kissed her lips. "I missed you."

Her fingers fluttered between them before settling delicately on his chest. "I missed you, too." Her mouth opened into a little *oh* at the admission, but she didn't look away. She owned her feelings, whether they were uncomfortable or not. He liked that. A lot.

"You look beautiful," he said, and meant every word.

"So do you," she admitted, then her eyes opened

wide. "Are you wearing *makeup*?" She laughed. "If only your teammates could see you now."

Roy frowned, then chuckled. Maybe he'd start a new trend.

PATIENCE HADN'T EXPECTED to find herself in Roy's arms, but now that she was... it was difficult to act naturally when her pulse had gone to the races and her girl parts were all aflutter. He'd said he missed her. She wanted to believe he was talking about more than their temporary partnership, that they had a chance together, but how could she trust her heart?

"Five minutes," a friendly young woman wearing a headset said, smiling when she saw them together.

Roy nodded, the humor dying an abrupt death, and the tech disappeared down the hall. His hands dropped away from her waist and he moved to close the door. Turning, he met Patience's steady gaze with panic. "I can't do this," he said.

Tenderness for the big, tough man blocking the door as though his life depended on it filled her with warmth. "Yes, you can. I'm going to be right there with you—well, behind the cameras, but it'll still be a friendly face in the room."

"I can't believe I let you talk me into this—I'm no TV star. I'm going to make a fool of myself."

Time to change the subject before he bailed on her. "Did the police contact you about Olivia?"

His head jerked. "No. Did they catch her?"

"Not yet, but Paul assured me it's only a matter of time. He wasn't supposed to say anything, but apparently, she trashed a hotel room on the edge of town. The guests in the next room heard the commotion and called the front desk. When the manager opened the door, he found the mirror smashed on the floor. The police were called in and they tied it to Olivia. She was there with another man, Roy." Patience tried to gauge if he was upset by the news, but his frown could mean anything.

"I should have handled the situation with her better. If I'd talked to her more..."

"Don't. You can't go second-guessing her motives. This is on Olivia. She needs help." Hopefully, before someone got hurt.

Roy glanced at the expensive watch on his wrist and sighed. "I guess my time is up. Let's get this over with."

Patience checked on Thomas again. Still sleeping. She'd read up on cats who'd been neutered; it usually took them a few days to recover and it was crucial to keep them from jumping as much as possible. Good luck with that. She smiled as she straightened and joined Roy at the door. "I'm sure the producers appreciate your excitement. Come on, it won't be that bad. I hear Sandra Bullock is on after you. Maybe you can get an autograph."

Roy's brow lifted. "Well, in that case—"

"I knew it," she crowed. "Mention a beautiful movie star and all of a sudden it's all sunshine and lollipops. Men, they're so predictable."

Roy grasped her arm, slowing their progress down the surprisingly quiet hall. "Thanks," he said, his eyes warm as they swept over her upturned face. "I don't feel like a cat on a hot tin roof anymore—sorry for the reference, Trouble."

Patience brushed an errant curl off his forehead. Tenderness and something dangerous filled her chest, making it hard to stay light and easy like he needed right now. "It's Thomas, and by the way, it's my week for custody." She smiled. "Okay, knock 'em dead out there."

"Is that anything like break a leg?" he asked, just as the tech rounded the corner and ushered him forward. He stood quietly as she attached a mic to his shirt and made a few comments on protocol. And then, with a last glance at Patience, he allowed himself to be led away.

19

Olivia hovered off-stage, careful to keep the station cap she'd *borrowed* over her eyes. It had been ridiculously easy to enter the building this morning under guise as a replacement hair stylist for the stars. Security waved her through with barely a glance at her forged ID card and she'd followed the crowd up to the eighth floor where the show was being filmed.

It was lucky she'd gone to that bar with the intention of drowning her sorrows after that run-in with Roy's... mistake. The woman was an overblown bimbo, for crying-out-loud. How could he even consider replacing Olivia with that... that slut? If not for the commercial announcing his upcoming interview, she would have been twiddling her thumbs in that backwater town while he returned to the city.

It didn't matter. She was here now, and soon, if things went to plan, they'd be together forever. She glanced beneath her lashes to the other side of the room where her brother hunkered behind a pile of boxes. She'd practically had to beg in order for him to cooperate, but without him her strategy for getting Roy alone would never work. She'd take care of her troublesome brother later.

Her heart catapulted into her throat when Roy suddenly appeared and took his place on stage to the left of the two talk-show hosts. He radiated tension, his shoulders stiff and brows lowered, but she seemed to be the only one who noticed. The woman on the dais—what was her name? Tanya Sullivan, that was it—smiled coyly and patted his knee like he was a damn dog, while her male counterpart scrolled his cell phone and ignored everyone.

Roy looked tired. Olivia hoped it wasn't her fault. She hadn't meant to get him benched. All she wanted was for them to have a second chance. Instead, she'd pushed him into the arms of another woman. She glared at the bitch, who seemed to be everywhere with Roy these days, and had to duck her head when the brunette turned to glance behind her—no doubt feeling the fictitious dagger in her back.

"Should be an interesting interview, huh?" A young guy with a goatee and a ponytail grinned at her as he moved his camera into place. "Did you hear the radio discussion the other day? Hockey players—all brawn and no brain."

As opposed to him, she guessed. Even as she smiled and nodded, Olivia pictured Roy slamming this milksop against the boards like an ant.

"You're new, aren't you? I haven't seen you around here." He leaned against the trolley carrying the heavy equipment and it started to roll away on him. He hurried to straighten and grasp the cart but lost a roll of electrical cord that fell to the floor with a solid thunk.

Shut up, you fool. She shot a desperate glance around them, relieved that other than the producer, who frowned at the imbecile, everyone else was focused on their jobs. "I'm a temp, yes. Looks like your boss needs you." She nodded toward the woman with a clipboard and a Pitbull stare.

He flushed and started to push the cart away. "Yeah, sure. Maybe we could meet up for a coffee sometime?"

Not likely. Olivia bared her teeth and nodded. "That would be great," she lied. Why would she think of going out with someone like *him* when she had her one true love? Or she would, soon.

"Good morning, we have a very special guest to share with you today," Tanya chirped. "NHL's bad boy, defenseman Roy Donaldson, winner of last year's

James Norris Memorial Trophy. Roy, welcome to the show."

Roy seemed to look right at Olivia as he smiled into the camera. She went weak in the knees and grasped a nearby desk for balance. She couldn't lose him, she just couldn't. He was the first man to ever treat her with respect. He didn't love her, she knew that. But with time...

"Glad to be here, though I have to admit I'd rather be playing hockey," he said, displaying some of the charm that had drawn her to him with such devastating effect.

"So, *Roy*, care to explain for our audience—and your fans—why you're not on the ice?" The other anchorman interjected.

You jackass. Olivia clenched her fists. That was between her and Roy, not the whole damn nation. This was her fault. If she'd kept her mouth shut and simply tried to contact Roy privately, none of this needed to happen.

The brunette shook her head and slid off the high stool they'd arranged for her, the white dress riding up her thighs. She tapped the producer on the arm and made a cut motion across her throat, but the Pitbull kept the cameras rolling.

Olivia stepped forward, instinctively reaching out to stop the torrent coming. But she was too late.

"You want to know why I'm here instead of playing the game I love? Fine, I'll tell you." Roy stared not at the camera, not at Olivia, but at the brunette with an intensity that stripped the room of any sound. "A woman I've come to like and respect once told me that the best way to represent myself was with the truth. The fact is, I've made mistakes—I'm sure we all have —" He glanced meaningfully at the male anchor before turning back to the woman in the white dress. "It's what we do after that that makes a difference. So, Olivia, if you're listening, call me. I want to help." He sat back, laced his hands in his lap, and the room gave a collective sigh.

The producer finally gave the signal to cut to break.

Olivia's heart was pounding, her hands sweaty. What should she do? Carry through with her plan or leave and trust Roy to do as he promised? She searched the shadows by the boxes for her brother, but there was no sign of him. Had he run off and left her to deal with this alone? *Dammit, Mike.* She had no choice; she'd have to leave.

Just then a hard, male hand gripped Olivia's arm. "RCMP. I'm sorry, ma'am, but you'll have to come with us."

Panicked, Olivia stared up at the officer and then around the room as plain clothes cops—including the goatee guy—blocked the exits and waited for orders from the man next to her. She was conscious of Roy rising and peering past the bright lighting, of the brunette looking at her with pity behind those horrendous green glasses, and Mike. He stood off to one side, a cop beside him, hands in cuffs and a guilty expression on his face. He'd done this. Turned on his own sister. How *could* he?

Enraged, she broke free and lunged for the personification of her grief—the brunette.

oy saw what was about to happen. He yelled at Patience to run as he sprang off the dais, but he was too late.

Olivia pulled a knife from her jacket and forced Patience to her knees. "Get down. Now, before I stick you with this," she screamed. Patience dropped, her eyes pleading with him to stay back. Olivia wrapped an arm around her neck and kept the one with the knife free. She was completely surrounded but for the moment, the advantage was hers.

"Let her go. You don't want to do this," he said, aware of the officers closing ranks. "Come on, Olivia, is it worth your freedom?"

She laughed while tears poured from her eyes. "That's rich, coming from you. You're so tied to that stupid sport; you didn't even see what was in front of you. *Me*," she cried. "All I wanted was for you to look at me, really look. And then *she* came along and I knew we were over." She tightened her hold on Patience's neck, forcing her head back and lifted the blade until it rested just under her jaw. "One cut and we could go back to what we were. It would be so easy." The knife nicked the skin and a fine line of red appeared. Blood.

The anchorwoman screeched somewhere behind Roy, but all he could see was Patience's big, terror-filled, brown eyes. Pulse pounding in his ears, he raised his hand, as he'd done the night he'd found the frightened cat, and eased closer. "I meant what I said back there; I really do want to help you. Talk to me, Olivia. Tell me what I can do."

She softened, just for a moment. Her arm loosened its hold and the blade eased away from Patience's throat, but then one of the idiots behind him stage-whispered, "I hope they have film rolling on this, it's dynamite." He shot the guy a venomous look, but the damage was done. Olivia stuck the knife under Patience's ribs and forced her back to her feet.

"It's too late for conversations, you had your chance. Now tell everyone to get out of my way or your girlfriend here is going to ruin her pretty dress." Because they were close to the same height, Olivia couldn't maintain her chokehold, so she grabbed

Patience by the hair and dragged her backward. "Oh, yeah, my brother comes with us. Let him go. Now."

Helpless, Roy tracked their awkward progress through the maze of cameras, cords and men, praying for a miracle. At any moment he expected to see that winking blade sink into Patience's side and a bright red bloom spread across the virginal white dress. He'd never been so scared—not even when his brother took his life. He hadn't been around to stop that tragedy, this was different. Patience could die today, and it was his fault. It was inconceivable, yet a sense of fatality told him it was all too real. If he didn't do something soon, Olivia and her brother would escape through that door and then Patience would become a hindrance— one they didn't need.

A grim nod from Paul set Olivia's brother free and he cautiously stepped around the officers to join the women. "Thanks, sis," he said, keeping a wary eye on the knife.

"Just do your job and help me get out of here," Olivia hissed, her anxiety palpable.

"If you walk through that door, there's no going back," Paul warned. "Kidnapping is a federal offence, Olivia. Do you *want* to raise your child in prison?"

The baby. Roy had forgotten her allegations what with everything else that was going on.

"Except there is no baby, is there, Olivia?"

Patience's voice rang out, strained but clear. "It was just a ploy. Is that really how you would want Roy back —out of guilt?"

"Shut up," Olivia shouted, yanking Patience's head around like a ragdoll. "You don't know anything. None of you do."

She was unraveling. They needed to do something, and fast. Roy glanced at Paul from the corner of his eye and noticed him making low hand signals to his men. Time to create a distraction.

"Olivia, if you let her go, I promise we can put this all behind us, okay? I shouldn't have broke things off the way I did. I'm truly sorry and want to make it up to you. Will you give me a chance?" Roy took a few careful steps forward, keeping her attention on him instead of the rangy goatee guy closing in on her from behind.

She stared at him with her heart in her eyes. "Do you mean it, Roy? That's all I'm asking for—a cha..."

"Look out," her brother cried, reaching out to jerk her away from the plainclothes officer. Olivia, thinking herself under attack, swung the blade, burying it in Mike's stomach.

Time froze.

He looked at her, shocked, then down at the hilt of the knife and the blood darkening his navy-blue t-shirt.

His hands cradled the wound as his knees gave out and he sank to the floor in slow motion.

Olivia stared at what she'd done, hands covering her mouth as mewling cries erupted from her throat. She dropped down beside him and cradled his head, tears running down her face. "I'm sorry. I'm so sorry," she chanted, rocking back and forth.

"Call emergency services," Paul yelled, skidding up to them the same time as Roy arrived.

Patience hiked up her skirt and knelt beside Olivia, stopping Roy's heart. "We need to pack the wound," she said, smiling gratefully when Roy yanked his shirt over his head. "Olivia. Olivia, let me help. My brother is a paramedic, he made sure we all got our basic first aid." She hugged her enemy in reassurance. "He's going to be fine, honey. Help is on the way." She carefully wrapped Roy's shirt around the knife and applied gentle pressure. "Hold his hand, he needs you."

Olivia looked at her with blank eyes, then lifted her gaze to Roy. "What have I done?" she whimpered. "Dear Lord, did I just kill my brother?"

"You keep crying on my face like that, you will," Mike grumbled. He cracked his eyes open around a grimace of pain. "It was an accident, sis. Hell, I probably deserved it for turning you in like that. I just wanted you to get help— you know, for your head. Are you mad at me?"

Olivia wiped her cheeks and leaned down to kiss his pasty forehead. "Not anymore," she whispered. "Not anymore."

Roy's throat closed up. If not for the grace of God, that could be Patience lying there with a knife sticking out—he shuddered. He wasn't sure when it had happened, but he was head over heels in love with his PA.

21

Patience stared at the emergency room doors, willing the doctor to come through them with good news about Olivia's brother. Her throat was still numb from the stitches she'd received, but she had a feeling it would be tender for a few days after the freezing came out. Not as sore as Mike, though.

When the paramedics arrived at the television station, Paul had ordered her to go in the ambulance with Mike, so she could be checked out. She'd reluctantly agreed, but only to ease his mind while he took Olivia—under arrest--in for questioning. With all the drama she'd lost sight of Roy and though she'd searched, he'd disappeared.

She turned her clean hands over—the sticky blood gone, but not forgotten. She never thought she'd have empathy for the woman who'd caused Roy so much misery, but the broken look on Olivia's face after the accident would stay with her for a long time.

It's the reason she was here now. If it were her brother lying on an operating table Patience would hope someone was there, so they weren't all alone. She would be that person for Mike.

The entrance doors whooshed open and her heart jumped, but instead of Roy, her parents, Marco, Linda and Tammy swarmed the foyer, panicked gazes searching the waiting room until they landed on her.

"Patience Kennedy, what have you gotten yourself into?" her mom cried, hands flapping as she scurried across the floor, dodging sick and weary people and one very patient service dog. "*Mamma mia*, my baby is injured."

"I'm fine, Mom. It's just a scratch." Patience tried not to flinch while her mother inspected the bandage. "How did you guys know I was here?"

"My buddy brought you in," Marco said, hands on hips. "But he wouldn't have needed to, *if you'd called home*."

Tammy pushed past him. "Leave your sister alone, can't you see she's hurt?" She grasped Patience's hand and squeezed. "He's right though, you should have called me."

Patience's dad stepped in to give her a hug that

smelled of fresh-baked bread, rosemary and oregano. "How's my baby-girl?"

She closed her eyes, inhaling the essence of home and hearth, and swallowed on a deep well of tenderness for her family and friends. "Love you, Daddy."

He patted her shoulder with a heavy hand and moved back to wipe damp eyes. "You gave us a scare, *figlia.*"

Patience nodded, ashamed, though it wasn't her fault. She looked at Linda. "I guess I screwed up, boss."

Linda's smile was perfunctory. "As long as you're all right, that's what matters," she said, quiet in the face of her family's support. "We'll talk when you're back to work."

"Leave her alone, Lins," Tammy warned. "Sometimes, I don't know how we became sisters."

"Well, if you need a lesson—" Marco interjected, a teasing glint in his eye.

"Ignore him, Tammy, he left his manners at home," Momma said, swatting his arm.

Family; they were a haven when times were rough, supportive, loyal and caring—a blessing.

"What happened? We heard something about an assault on the radio coming down here, but there weren't many details." Linda took a chair across from her and leaned forward. "Where is Mr. Donaldson?"

"The hockey player, that Donaldson?" Marco's

ears perked up. "Is that who you were mooning over that day you hurt your ankle?"

Even as she glared at her brother, Patience couldn't believe how much had happened since then. "Careful, I didn't give you those tickets yet."

"Well, if you have a young man in your life, he should be here," her mother said, thick brows pleated in annoyance.

"He's not my—"

"I'm sorry I'm late," Roy said, striding into the midst of the Kennedy clan like a soldier on a white horse. "Your brother insisted I take a side trip down to the police station before coming here." He crouched at her feet and clasped her hands. "How are you?"

Her heart fluttered like a crazed bird against the wall of her chest. He was looking at her with so much warmth and tenderness that she promptly forgave him for disappearing at the TV station. "I'm okay." *Now that you're here.* "It was kind of crazy back there."

He squeezed her fingers. "When I saw that knife—"

"Knife?" her mother cried, paling. "What knife?"

Patience cringed. "Can we talk about that later?" she asked, aware of the curious gazes they were attracting. "No one was seriously hurt, Mom. See?" She wiggled her fingers. "All my fingers and toes are where they should be."

"Always the comedian," her mother huffed, sinking into a chair. "Why are the parents always the last to know?"

"Because we love you, that's why," Marco said, wrapping an arm around her shoulders to draw her close. "We don't want you to worry."

"We're parents," Dad said. "It's what we do." He wiped his eyes and nose with a cloth hankie and shoved it in his pocket. "Now introduce us to your beau."

Patience was sure her face was as red as her hands had been earlier. She met Roy's bemused gaze and gave a helpless shrug. She'd tried; as usual her family heard what they wanted to hear—God bless them.

"Mom, Dad, this is Roy Donaldson. I've been trying, not very well, to help him with his social media presence and we became... friends."

Roy raised his brow, calling her bluff. He rose and shook her father's hand and smiled at her mother. "I think what your daughter is saying in a roundabout way is that we're interested in dating." He met Patience's wide-eyed gaze and grinned. "That is if she doesn't mind being my permanent personal assistant?"

She blushed fiery red, quite sure he wasn't talking about work. "I suppose we could negotiate terms," she said and threw herself into his arms. The PA and the hockey player; who would have imagined?

EPILOGUE

One year later

Roy held his position as a wall of red barreled down the ice toward the WarHawks goal net. His pulse pounded in anticipation of the clash between warriors of the Flames and their team. The game was tied in overtime—it was do or die.

A quick glance back revealed the goalie, Cole Reed, braced for impact, a shit-eating grin noticeable even through his full-face mask. They lived for this, all of them. Adrenaline coursing through their veins, the roar of the crowd, the competitive spirit that pushed them beyond most men's limits.

This was the last game before playoffs. They needed it to secure their spot in the race for the Stanley Cup—the ultimate goal for any hockey player.

Lazlo broke through the ranks, racing to get in the way of the carnage about to descend on Roy's head. They'd been caught off-guard, but that didn't stop his team from doing everything short of building an impenetrable wall around the net to stop the probable outcome.

The Calgary team were well-known for their aggressive forward passes and they'd seen this throughout the game. For his team's part, they'd played a defensive strategy and it had worked out well, until now. With the rest of the WarHawks playing catch-up from the back of the pack, the pressure was on.

Their wingman passed the puck just before he rammed up against the mountain that was Lazlo. It flew across the ice and came to rest against the center's stick. Roy knew he only had one chance to make a difference. He counted off the seconds in his head, laser-focused on the opposing team captain. The moment the man's arm moved, he lunged to stop the puck's trajectory. Using every inch of reach he could muster, Roy caught the puck with the tip of his stick, sending it ricocheting off the boards and into the waiting hands of Cooper. Coop snapped off a lightning-fast backward pass to Wanowski on center line and he took off straight for their goaltender, winging the puck right past the guy's head and into the net. The buzzer sounded and the crowd went wild.

After a whole bunch of hell-yeahs and knock-your-teeth-out back-slapping, they lined up and shook the Flames hands, congratulating them on a good game before slowly making their way off-ice.

Roy was near the back of the group and glanced up at the stands, hoping to see Patience among the well-wishers. It was a sea of black, many of their fans wearing team colors. He was about to give up when he saw it. A red and white teddy bear with the words *Be Mine* engraved on a heart-shaped pillow and the woman waving it in front of her like a crazed lunatic. His fiancée and soon-to-be-bride caught his eye and grinned before throwing the bear onto the ice at his feet.

Smiling, he picked it up and raised it in the air for all to see. He'd scored the biggest prize of all—true love.

Chapter One

Holly Tremaine glared after the cabbie who'd just

driven away with her carefully wrapped Christmas gifts in the backseat. She'd done everything short of flying to catch his attention, all to no avail. Now what was she going to do? She hadn't even caught the number of his taxi. The car was blue and white, and the cab driver had been an older man with pictures of his two grandchildren taped to his dash—that's all the information she had.

What a mess.

The bluebird of lost hopes—aka the cab—disappeared into the busy Victoria traffic leaving Holly alone to face her past. She swallowed hard and turned toward her parents' imposing two-story townhouse. The dismal day blended with the gray stone and black iron accents that had intimidated her as a child—nice to see some things remained the same.

Sighing, she tightened her grip on the carry-on bag she'd limited herself to for the flight—which is why she was now giftless—and trudged toward the big oak doors as though she were fighting her way through quicksand. Great. Not even in the house and she already regretted the trip.

The sign below the bell was no less glaring for the elegant script; No Soliciting, Fundraising, Salesmen, Religion or Politics- Thank you.

As though attaching manners at the end softened

the cold tone the message conveyed. That was her parents in a nutshell.

She jabbed the bell like it was a release valve for her frustration. The rain that had held off while she dashed from store to store began to fall—a misty drizzle that sank into Holly's clothes and turned her hair lank in a matter of seconds. Wet and miserable, she waited for someone to let her in.

The door swung back revealing a yawning black maw—or so it seemed in that moment. The one person Holly had hoped to avoid stood in the entry.

Her sister.

"Holly." Susan looked down her slender, too perfect, nose. "You're late."

Holly blew a wayward strand of wet hair away from her face and tried to ignore the tic developing over her right eyebrow. "Well, I'm here now. Better late than never, right?" She glanced over her shoulder at the curtain of rain. "Mind letting me in? It's cold out here." She smiled and took a step forward, forcing her sister to move or get plowed down.

The grand entrance was just as inhospitable as she remembered. Dark wood climbed the walls while marble tile covered the floor like a layer of ice. Eight years and nothing had changed.

"Where are they?" she asked, though she knew the

answer by glancing at her watch. Five o'clock, time for pre-dinner drinks in the lounge.

"Mom and Dad? Or Steven?"

The nervous tap-tapping of Susan's glossy black pump told Holly she wasn't nearly as calm as she pretended. For her part, Holly couldn't control the fluttering in her stomach at the thought of seeing Steven after all these years. Her sister looked... older—harder. Maybe married life hadn't turned out like she expected. Was it wrong Holly hoped that was true?

"I just arrived, Sue." They'd both used nicknames for each other as children. "Can we save the arguing until tomorrow? I'm beat."

Susan's expression softened as though she, too, regretted the distance that had grown between them. "Hols, we need to..."

"Who was at the door, darling? Your parents are acting even stranger than normal." Steven approached from down the hall, his view obstructed by his wife.

Breathe, Holly. She was going to hyperventilate and embarrass herself by passing out on the floor at their feet, she could see it now. Well, she could if not for the black dots dancing before her eyes. *Oh man*, he was every bit as striking as she remembered. Movie star handsome. And at one time, the love of her life. No matter how many pep-talks she'd given herself, nothing could have prepared her for this.

Her vision blurred. She leaned hard on the handle of her luggage as her knees wobbled, then gasped as the wheels slipped out from under her and she went down, landing hard on her elbow.

"Ow," she muttered, almost as an afterthought, too busy trying to control her flip-flopping tummy. "I don't feel so good." At least the tiles were cool on her back—small favors.

"Take it easy," a rich, deep voice murmured. And then he was there. Warm hands cradled her head while wide shoulders blocked the vision of Susan's surprisingly worried expression. Strange, she thought Susan would be laughing at her predicament.

"I'm fine," she snapped, wriggling to escape Steven's hold. But then she looked into his eyes and froze. Steven's eyes were the blue of a midnight sky. These eyes matched the winter storm lashing the window panes—grim and steely. "You," she whispered, stunned.

"Were you hoping for someone else?" Steven's annoying, pain-in-her-butt brother asked.

Holly lay back and closed her eyes. "Why can't I catch a break?"

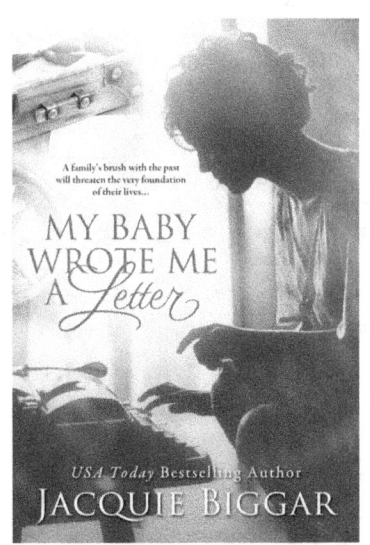

My Baby Wrote Me A Letter

A family's brush with the past will threaten the fabric of their lives.

Eight months pregnant and her Navy husband away on a mission, Grace Freeman craves the security of her childhood home in Canada.

When a letter written by her long-lost mother is found in an old writing desk it creates a tear in the fabric of her family.

Can Grace find a way to bring peace to those she loves, or will a message from the past destroy their future?

Newsletter subscribers also get bonus content and insider information every month. I love giveaways and there is lots of interesting stuff for me to share with you!

Newsletter- Sign up Now!

AFTERWORD

In 1879 the first organized team, the McGill University Hockey Club, was formed, and with the advent of a basic set of rules, the sport quickly spread across Canada. The first "world championship" was held in 1883 at the Montreal Ice Carnival and was won by McGill. Even though the winter carnival hockey tournament was considered a "world championship," only teams from Eastern Canada participated, according to the Montreal *Gazette*. The first national association, known as the Amateur Hockey Association of Canada, was formed in 1886, with representatives from Québec City, Montréal and Ottawa. A group of colleges, universities, and military and athletic clubs formed the Ontario Hockey Association in 1890. Governor General Lord Stanley donated a trophy in 1893 for the national championship, and the first Stanley Cup game was played 22 March 1893, with Montreal AAA victorious before a crowd of 5000.

Attribution:
https://www.thecanadianencyclopedia.ca/en/article/ice-hockey

ACKNOWLEDGMENTS

Reviews are the lifeblood of any successful author. Without you, we can't be heard.

If you enjoy the story, please consider sharing on your favorite social media sites, as well as GoodReads and from wherever you've bought the book.

Thank you,

Jacquie Biggar

Jacqbiggar.com

ABOUT THE AUTHOR

JACQUIE BIGGAR is a USA Today bestselling author of Romantic Suspense who loves to write about tough, alpha males and strong, contemporary women willing to show their men that true power comes from love.

She is the author of the popular Wounded Hearts series and has just started a new series in paranormal suspense, Mended Souls.

She has been blessed with a long, happy marriage and enjoys writing romance novels that end with happily-ever-afters.

Jacquie lives in paradise along the west coast of

Canada with her family and loves reading, writing, and flower gardening. She swears she can't function without coffee, preferably at the beach with her sweetheart. :)

Sign up now to keep up with Jacquie's new releases, excerpts, giveaways, and more:

Newsletter

jacqbiggar.com
jbiggar@jacqbiggar.com

My Girl

Married to The Texan- Box set

BLUE HAVEN

Sweetheart Cove

Sunset Beach

MEN OF WARHAWKS

Skating on Thin Ice

The Player

SINGLE TITLES

Silver Bells

The Lady Said No

My Baby Wrote Me A Letter

Tempted by Mr. Wrong

Valentine: A Hearts and Kisses Romance

Mistletoe Inn

The Sister Pact